SPIRItS

AMONG US

SHERRY HOWARD

REYCRAFT
BOOKS

Reycraft Books
55 Fifth Avenue
New York, NY 10003

Reycraftbooks.com

Reycraft Books is a trade imprint and trademark of Newmark Learning, LLC.

Library of Congress Control Number 2020910356

ISBN: 978-1-4788-7027-2

Printed in Dongguan, China. 8557/0620/17230

10 9 8 7 6 5 4 3 2 1

First Edition Hardcover published by Reycraft Books 2020

Reycraft Books and Newmark Learning, LLC, support diversity and
the First Amendment, and celebrate the right to read.

To Mom and Dad,
who taught me to be strong
in a body with weaknesses.

—SHERRY HOWARD

CONTENTS

CHAPTER ONE

Before I lost Momma, a year seemed to last forever. A year was ticking away now, and I needed to connect with Momma before it was over. I bit my lip and prayed for a miracle.

"You okay, Scooter?" Harlan, my best friend since first grade, six years now, broke the silence after a bit.

I handed the flowers to him and he put them on Momma's grave, in the vase that stayed here forever, just like Momma. My heavy wheelchair wouldn't get me near Momma's stone. My chest tightened like my heart was being squeezed, preventing me from answering, but Harlan surely understood. He'd been stuck to my side like superglue since the accident nearly a year ago. That could be annoying to me once in a while, but mostly I reckon it was a good thing. My wheelchair didn't stop me from doing much, but when it did, Harlan made things work out okay.

Tombstones surrounded us on all sides. Some tall and fancy, some tiny plaques in the dirt for babies. That might have freaked some kids out—to be inside a fence with only tombstones for company. Not Harlan and me. To us, they were as much a part of life as fog over the hollow, something to study. A sign that you were never really gone—as long as people didn't forget. Our town—this holler—called Chamber's Corner after my first relative to settle here, respected spirits. Our property was known to be blessed with folks who'd passed on but hung around for a good long haunting. It must be hard to leave behind this place and the people who made it seem like a little corner of paradise—most of the time, anyway.

Some of the granite tombstones sparkled like fairy dust had been sprinkled on them. Not Momma's stone though. Her pink headstone had no sparkle, which didn't seem fair, since she had more sparkle than anybody. I forced down the tears that tried to spring up. No sign from Momma today. The birds chirped and her garden blossomed outside the gates. I sat as still as I could. Only the light breeze whistled through the woods. Down in this Appalachian hollow, the beautiful mountains kept us in a hug of quiet with only a sprinkle of light wind allowed in.

If only a bird or butterfly would land on Momma's headstone. She'd give me a sign soon.

Every week when we went to Momma's grave, we waited for her spirit to visit us—our biggest wish. She knew how to make herself known to us—a bird, a butterfly, something that wouldn't let us look away. After all, she'd been an expert ghost hunter herself—not ghosts like the white-sheeted kind, but spirits, the part of us that remains after our bodies give out.

"It's past time," I grumbled. Max, my chocolate lab and the best dog in the known universe, licked my hand. I rubbed the butterfly on my necklace. The last present Momma gave me.

"Be patient. She'll visit us when she can," Harlan said. "A year ain't all that long for crossing over."

"Ha! Patience! You know if she doesn't make it soon, she might never make it at all. So, do you still feel her here, or is it just me?" Mountain legend had it that if you didn't hear from a spirit that first year, they might get too far away to reach you anymore.

I pulled petals from the black-eyed Susan I'd kept from the bouquet. Harlan's momma had taken off not long after he was born, and he'd loved Momma a lot, so it seemed right that he'd feel her too.

"I do. But I sort of feel her in a lot of places." Harlan fooled around with the flowers until he grinned, stood up, and nodded his head. He had a good eye for making things look special. Guess that's why he was a great photographer.

"Me, too. But mostly here. And in her butterfly garden." By now the petals of the black-eyed Susan from Momma's garden had told me Momma wouldn't visit today. I'd peeled the petals off one by one. She'll visit, she'll visit not. . . . Some days the petals said she'd visit, some days not. No matter what the flowers said, she still hadn't made herself known to us. At least not in a way that we could tell.

She would someday. I had to believe in that.

The names on the markers showed a roll call of family who'd lived and died on this land we called Chamber's Creek, known as one of the most haunted spots in the United States. Like iron to a magnet, I gravitated to Zebediah's massive headstone, one of the first placed here.

I ran my fingers across the letters of his name, the numbers of his birth date. "How'd this dirt get so messed up in only a week?" Something must've been digging out here, in the grass over his grave. No person would desecrate a grave, would they?

Harlan trimmed the grass with the clippers we always carried to the cemetery. "Hmmm. Maybe critters? Have you seen snakes? I'd like to catch me a snake."

"I finished my research on Zebediah. We should be ready to add to our feature on him, especially how he bought this land." I had spent weeks going over Momma's notes on Zeb, getting ready for our YouTube show on him.

"We added fifty subscribers last week," Harlan said. "We must be doing something right."

Our YouTube channel, *Spirits Among Us,* had passed 10,000 subscribers, and now exploded with new followers after every post. Word was getting around.

Our town was a famous hotspot for ghost hunters, and Momma had been a well-known ghost hunter. We'd used her research on hot spots around the country to start our channel. She had helped us get it going not long before the accident.

Harlan, Max, and I basked in the Kentucky sunshine a few minutes. Sun glinted off the front windows of the abandoned bus outside the cemetery fence—the only windows Dad hadn't accidentally hit when he splatter-painted that and our van. We hadn't played on that old thing in a long time—not since Dad caught us the last time and grounded me for two weeks after I got stuck on it in my wheelchair. The lift on that bus was as stubborn as a Missouri mule; it worked only when it wanted to.

I bowed my head and inhaled the sweet smell of Kentucky bluegrass—enjoying a bit of quiet before Harlan's uncle picked him up. Max snuggled against Harlan, who gave endless belly rubs.

"Smells like sunshine." Harlan kept up the belly rubs on Max, who glanced at Harlan with pure puppy love.

"And grass," I grinned. "Maybe a little dog smell too. You must've used your deodorant today."

Harlan threw a clod of dirt at me. But he grinned.

A sudden flash of color in the woods across the field signaled we had company. I squinted against the sun, but whatever it was disappeared among the brush and trees. Another flash of yellow appeared deeper in the woods, as if running away.

"Did you see that?" I asked. Max whimpered at my feet. Why didn't he chase after it? He chased *everything*.

"What?" Harlan's gaze followed my finger to the woods.

"In the woods. Somebody. Something." I shaded my eyes and stared, but nothing moved.

"Probably some ghost hunter trying to find the cemetery," Harlan said with his usual logic. He shrugged.

"Let's check it out," I said. "Come on."

He glanced at his watch. "No time. Uncle Sonny will be here in fifteen. Time to head back."

"Hmmm. Nobody should be back here." My insides quivered. I grabbed my notebook from the pouch beside me and jotted a quick note: *Something moved in the woods. Saw a flash of yellow, like Momma's favorite shirt. I'll leave her a message.*

I'd be sure to ask Dad if he'd sent anybody out that way. Something felt off. Seemed like a legit visitor would've spoken to us. Surely Momma wouldn't have run away from us. I dropped my tiny lucky Yoda figure in the grass, so she'd understand I'd seen her. Just in case.

CHAPTER TWO

Sweat trickled down my back, soaking my shirt while I waited to intercept our mail lady at the far end of our long driveway. Hurry up, Julia!

Fourteen days ago, I'd plunked down my life savings to buy a special camera. For the last week, I'd tracked it online to see when it would arrive. The days ticked slower than a turtle crossing the road in front of your car. When they say seven to fourteen days, you might as well count on fourteen.

"Expecting mail today, Scooter?" Julia grinned, then scooped something up from the seat beside her.

"Is there something for me?" I kept my voice calm and neutral, but inside I was jumping up and down clapping.

"Here ya go." She leaned out her window and handed me a stack of mail in white envelopes, like bills and stuff.

I swallowed my disappointment. Tomorrow would be another day of sneaking mail into the house.

She waited for what felt like a minute of torture, grinned, then handed over a package with my name on it. "Girl, you will fry yourself to a crisp in this hot sun. Get inside!"

My heart raced while I thanked her. This might be the key to finding Momma's spirit. At least it would get me started and keep me distracted so I didn't have to miss her every minute of every day. If the old folks of the holler were right, time was running out for Momma. I had to make it easy for her to reach me.

I hugged the brown package. Yes! Finally! My own camera with thermal imaging, solar recharge, and a high capacity battery. The best ghost hunting camera that I could buy. I *might've* spent the money I'd been saving for back-to-school clothes and shoes. And all my other savings, too. And borrowed a little from Uncle Ezra.

When I'd ordered the camera online, I'd done the research, used my PayPal account that Dad had set up for video app and online purchases, and then hoped for the best. Hopefully, Dad wouldn't be checking my bank balance any time soon.

Two weeks had been a long time to wait to see if I'd gotten ripped off. What if I'd wasted all that money on a scam? Maybe the camera would be a scam, but at least *something* had arrived.

Nobody knew I'd ordered this, not even Harlan. I savored my little secret, patting the box like a calico kitten. I pictured the look on Harlan's face when I showed him this great new investment for our spirit search.

I left the rest of the mail on the table inside the front door and made it to my room without anybody noticing. Max, slobbery wet from slurping water, bounded onto my bed, closed his eyes, and relaxed. I put the box on my desk.

Should I open the package or wait for Harlan? My fingers itched to tear off the tape and drag out the camera. But Harlan was my official partner, and I might hurt his feelings if I bought and paid for it AND opened it without him. He'd be as excited as I was, and I wanted to see that in person. Wait for him, it was. I tucked the box under my bed, hoping Gran didn't go on a cleaning spree searching for dust bunnies any time soon. You never knew what Gran might be up to.

Since Momma died, the why and even the how of spirits lingering around us on Earth meant a lot more to me. Like, what if a person didn't get to tell someone goodbye? Would their spirit hang around a while until they found a way to say it? Would they be restless and sad until they could reach out? I had to make it easy as a sweet whisper for Momma to tell me goodbye.

CHAPTER THREE

I glanced to where the package waited under my bed. I wanted more than anything to open the package and see what I had to work with now, if it was the cool camera the Internet told me it would be. Instead, I grabbed a pen and wrote in the spirit log:

The camera arrived today! Soon we'll have recordings of our cemetery. This camera will finally give us some proof of our own. The ghost hunters who'd been here for the TV coverage years ago had only gotten grainy images. That was before I was born, and equipment wasn't as good. Harlan and I will set this up soon, and capture spirits, hopefully Momma, maybe Zebediah, since he's supposed to be the main haunt here. Everyone says he shows himself pretty often by leaving feathers that appear from nowhere, and by showing up as a warm spot in the air around the cemetery. And random pennies we find all over the property. Things like that.

"Scooter Marie! Dinner!" Dad's voice snapped, like he'd already called me a couple of times.

I pushed aside my journal and my reference book, *The Girl's Ghost Hunting Guide*. I'd finish my daily entry and do more research later.

I hurried to the kitchen. I tried to be careful— our walls and woodwork were dinged with marks since I didn't always calculate my turns very well. I reckoned I'd better study hard whatever math calls for figuring out distance.

Max followed me. His tail wagged in anticipation of some dinnertime treats under the table, forbidden now by Gran, but I could be sneaky when I needed to be.

"You know I expect you to come the first time I call." Dad's Marine background came through every now and then.

"Sorry." I swung into place at the table.

Supper at our old farmhouse could go from stuffy to silly in three seconds flat. And tonight, it did. Silverware gleamed and perfectly pressed napkins waited while Gran called down a nod from above for all the blessings we had in our lives, which she listed in detail. The second she uttered her heartfelt *Amen*, Max howled, long and loud. What in tarnation?

Uncle Ezra widened his eyes, all innocent-like, "You been teaching that dog new tricks? Scooter, I'm shocked you'd teach that dog such disrespect." He winked, and I stifled my laugh with my napkin.

I shushed Max before Gran could banish him from the kitchen for the thousandth time. Uncle Ezra got me and Max in a good deal of trouble, but we never told on him. He'd do about anything to make us laugh. He called himself the entertainment committee of Chamber's Creek. Dad called himself the mayor.

I'd seen Uncle Ezra training Max in his howling skills over the last few weeks but hadn't known that Gran and the Good Lord would be the punchline.

Dad chuckled. "This chicken and dumplings is the best you've ever made, Gran. You'd take a blue ribbon in a county fair."

"That's right." Uncle Ezra patted his flat belly. "We starved until you came along to feed us. Don't you think we need fattening up?" Flattery derailed Gran's anger every time, and her precious twins, Dad and Uncle Ezra, knew it.

Max behaved himself for the rest of the meal, with a little help from the pieces of chicken I slipped him. He'd adjusted to Gran joining our household better than I had. Uncle Ezra left his little apartment behind and moved in to help first after Momma died, then Gran followed him a few months later, leaving her house empty for the time being. Her plan was to stay with us only as long as we needed her—I think she was afraid of overstaying her welcome. Besides, her restaurant in town kept her super busy. In the mountains, family was everything, and your people rallied in times of trouble.

"Remember the time Mr. Thompson called Gran in because he was sure we were lying about which one of us was which?" Dad grinned at the memory.

"Those new haircuts sure did the job. I knew we could trip him up. He always was a pushover." Uncle Ezra winked at me. "Even worked on Gran for a few minutes that time."

I wished I had a twin—too many grown-ups around here. With Momma gone and Dad so broke up it seemed pretty unlikely now that I'd ever have a brother or sister. I'd better stay friends with Harlan so we could be old together. He was as good as a brother anyway, maybe better.

"Scooter," Gran said, "don't you pay any attention to such silliness. Are you ready for some pie, baby girl?" She focused her full attention on me—she could only stand so much silliness before she got flustered. "Your momma would be so proud of you, Scooter Marie, if she could see you now, such a little lady."

"Momma does see me. She does." Tears threatened to explode. Ever since Momma died before I could tell her goodbye, I'd become the worst crying crybaby on the entire planet, and possibly Mars. I was only twelve—I needed my Momma.

"May I be excused?" It seemed they all held their breath about half the time, worried about me, the crying crybaby. Sometimes, I got tired of trying to hide my sadness. I was eat up with the blues but had to swallow it down. How could life possibly be normal without Momma in it?

I left the table without waiting for an answer, trailed by Max. Even though Gran would probably end up crying herself, I had Momma too heavy in my heart right now to pretend Gran's comment didn't hurt, or to worry about her hurt feelings.

I sat on the porch. The sunset spread a cotton candy spray of pink across the sky. A distant rumble of thunder predicted a storm rolling in soon. I pulled out my journal. *I wish people would believe in Momma's spirit. She **is** all around me—I **know** she is. Please, Momma, prove it so they'll believe too.*

I pushed down all the pain and locked it away for now. I picked up my guitar and strummed a few of my favorite sad songs, hugging the sadness around me like a patchwork quilt.

Smoke hung over the mountains in wispy shapes. Maybe that's why we believe in spirits so much around here. Lots of days it looks like spirits are rising up out of the mountains. Maybe Momma was out there tonight in the mist. Soon she'd find a way to let us know. I needed to get away before anybody came to check up on me.

I'd go work on some posts for our YouTube channel, *Spirits Among Us*, and try not to think about Momma for a while. Searching for other spirits kept me busy while I waited for Momma to come. Harlan and I had a strong following, and we had to post weekly or we'd lose followers. Planning our next post would take my mind off my worries. Halloween was only two months away, and we had big plans for a special post. Maybe we'd even have film by then.

Soon we could set up our new camera and catch some spirits on film. Maybe even Momma.

CHAPTER FOUR

I paused at the doorway to my room. Something about my room seemed different—a little off. Yoda—check. Yoda still reigned supreme among my Star Wars collection on the shelves. Basketball trophies—check, still there. Books beside my bed and on it—check. Nothing seemed to be missing. Max stayed by my side in the doorway—even he felt it. He usually bounded into my room ahead of me and hopped onto the bed. The air thickened—heavy. Still, I couldn't put my finger on whatever it was that was off. Maybe tonight's mists had spooked me.

Then my quiet room came to life like a scene from Beetlejuice, that old movie Dad loves, where spirits make people move. I shivered while my room lit up. I put my hand on Max, who whimpered at my side.

Zigzag stripes of static whizzed across my television screen. Electrical current popped along the lamp cord, up the base, and around the lamp shade. Flickering lights animated my bedroom, while Journey's "Don't Stop Believin'" blasted from the oldies station on the clock radio at the bedside. A tickle of electricity flashed through me!

I remembered to breathe and tried to take it all in. Amazing! And beautiful! Maybe a little scary. What was happening here? I blinked as the room stilled.

My bedside light flickered off and on three times and then stayed on. Goosebumps crawled up my arms and I took another deep breath. Beside me, Max lay down and whimpered louder, an eighty-pound sissy, not about to go into my room. If I'd had a lick of sense, I'd have been lickety-split out of there. But I had a feeling, a pull, like someone had important news.

I whispered, "Zeb?" and waited. That's what you're supposed to do when you think a spirit is a light, or friendly, spirit. Call them by name and wait. They might be trying to tell you something. I'd touched Zeb's headstone, shown him respect. Maybe he needed to communicate and trusted me. The dirt had been messed up around him, and maybe there was a reason.

I didn't think my heart could race any faster, but it did. My computer screen flashed blue light and one of my videos showed—not the last screen I'd used when I shut down the computer before dinner. Instead, Zeb's tombstone filled the monitor. A shot I'd filmed for the YouTube video we were working on. I smiled and nodded at the answer. Chills chased up my spine. He actually answered me.

I had hoped Zeb would show up somehow today; it was his 175th birthday after all. I didn't expect him to make such a flash though. It was almost like he was upset about something. We knew him as a peaceful spirit around here. He'd been said to haunt our property for years, but he'd never been known to come into the house.

Zeb had been a strong character in our family history, a guy who'd died and left behind a lot of kids. Zebediah became one of the first

Kentuckians to free his slaves, long before he came home in 1865 after fighting for the Union, changed forever after fighting side-by-side with his darker-skinned soldiers. Gentlemen he considered true brothers. He was a respected landowner who went against what society expected and stood for what he believed.

The electric light show had stopped as suddenly as it had started. I'd barely pulled myself together and reached for my phone to snap a picture before it all disappeared in one last flash. Crap!

I lingered in the doorway, goosebumps dimpling my arms and Max whining softly now. It might have been seconds or minutes or days. I snapped out of it.

The music from the radio had disappeared with the last flash. "Don't Stop Believin'" had been Momma's favorite song. Memories of her dancing to it flashed in my muddled brain.

I reran the scene through my thoughts. Had it really happened or had my imagination gone totally crazy? It would've been nice to be faster with my phone. I almost needed to prove it to myself. Had my brain taken flight like a pack of pigeons chased by a hound? But proof enough was Max still whimpering at my side. I patted him and soothed his ruffled fur.

I'd wanted to see physical proof of our haint—that's country for ghost. I'd been told all my life that our house and business were haunted. I'd felt our spirits. Momma had told me a million stories of haunts. We'd found signs from Zeb, pennies and feathers that floated right into our laps. But this—this was something else.

Now I'd *seen* Zebediah, and maybe he'd brought me a tiny message from Momma through that song. Maybe Momma's spirit lingered, half in this world and half in the next. Maybe right now this was the only way she could reach us. Maybe she really needed me to help her cross over.

I raced into my room and over to my desk. The computer screen still showed Zebediah's tombstone. I'd known Zeb would like the story about him that Harlan and I were working on for our channel. His headstone, with a lion, was one of the most beautiful I'd ever seen, and I'd visited a lot of cemeteries with Momma for her ghost hunting.

Harlan. I had to tell Harlan! He'd believe me. I didn't think anyone else would. My room looked perfectly normal now. Dad, Uncle Ezra, and Gran would have a million reasons why it couldn't have happened the way I saw it. Or, they'd humor me, which I'd hate even more. Especially after how upset I'd been at dinner.

I fumbled my phone, nearly dropping it in my rush to share the news with Harlan. The light show I'd just witnessed in my room—even though I couldn't get the picture—*proved* dead people could communicate with living people. I'd never come this close to having physical proof. So close. I wished I could tell him in person, but I couldn't wait. I wished I could hear his voice. Harlan couldn't have phone calls because his dad was really strict. He worked a lot of extra shifts at the mines and slept whenever he could. Harlan had to be super quiet in his house.

I texted him.

He's been here.

Who? Harlan answered right away. Good. Harlan could talk.

Zeb.

You mean tombstone Zeb? How do u no?

Lights flickered, more stuff. I felt him.

For real? Gr8!

Yes, real. Thrilled!

Awesome. Get a pic?

Nope. Gone too fast.

Take notes for the journal?

Not yet. I will.

Can't wait to hear all about it.

I think he brought a message from Momma.

How?

Song that played right when he was here.

What song?

"Don't Stop Believin'." Her fave.

Wow!

Gotta go write journal. Ttyl.

K. Ttyl. Can't wait to hear more.

I made detailed notes in our spirit journal before I forgot everything. I made a video that I'd share later on YouTube, after Harlan edited it. If only I'd been quicker, I might've gotten pictures. Next time I wouldn't let that happen. Next time, it could be Momma. This time, because it was his birthday, and he's our major haint, I was pretty sure it was Zeb. But I believed in my heart that he carried a message to me. I needed to figure out what the message was because that electric light show was pretty extreme—like he was mad about something, like he was tattling on someone. What could have made him so upset? Maybe the animals digging up around his plot?

That's the problem with spirit communications to the living—we don't speak the same language. Sort of like some people. Just because I don't understand someone speaking to me in French doesn't mean they aren't speaking—it just means I haven't learned how to interpret what they're saying. I think that's the exact problem with us understanding spirits—we can't interpret what they say even when they try hard to tell us something. I think that's why sometimes they send us messages through things, like leaving me the picture of his tombstone the way Zeb did, so I could be sure it was really him. Like the music, so I'd know Momma was okay.

Next thing I knew, Dad's footsteps echoed in the hallway. My mind still raced with possibilities for ways I could use other spirits to talk to Momma, to help her cross over. I couldn't possibly sleep now. But I tried to arrange my face to look all innocent and sleepy. Dad wouldn't understand. He'd probably say I imagined it all, or our old house had an electrical surge, or the storm outside reflected lightning into my room. But I knew better.

"Why's everything still on? It's late. You should be asleep." He walked around the room, turning off the desk lamp, the television. Instead of a lecture, he shook his head and gave me the stink eye. He turned back my Star Wars comforter and plumped my pillow.

"Are you ready?" He walked toward me at the desk.

"Cleared for landing." I held out my arms.

When he swept me up and swung me around before plopping me into the bed, I was flying, like I would never need my wheelchair again.

"Won't be able to do that much longer with this old back," he said, trying to hide his grin as he straightened up, huffing and wheezing in a cheap imitation of the real thing, while Max jumped in beside me.

I giggled. "Sure you will, Dad. You can't fool me." I expected he could hoist me for many more years—even when I wasn't a scrawny twelve-year-old. I could do the transfer to bed on my own, but I loved our ritual too much to give it up. It wouldn't be much longer, but right now he needed to be needed. And he was.

Our bedtime routine was the best part of my day since I got hurt in the same accident that killed Momma. We'd been driving along when BLAM, out of nowhere, a car slammed into us. The next thing I knew I woke up to bright lights and lots of faces hovering over me in the emergency room. I never got to tell Momma goodbye, and it must bother her so much that she didn't get one last butterfly kiss. Dad was my rock then, and now.

"Dad, do we have any big parties booked tomorrow?" My work at the family paintball business helped Dad and Uncle Ezra get the players on the field more quickly. Harlan and I were responsible for getting the players outfitted and supplied with paint. Gran was the only family member exempt from working in the business. I couldn't picture her being around all that chaos—she'd be praying over everybody and imposing order—where it wasn't wanted. Besides she had her pizza place in town to manage.

"Nope, regular opening time. You and Harlan need to man the paintball stations at eleven. I expect a busy day." Dad's brows furrowed when he saw my phone already in my hand. When Dad tried to be stern, he talked about taking my phone away after dinner, but he never did. I never pushed my luck though.

"Night then. Love you." I blew him a last kiss. Max snuggled closer, nice and warm.

"Love you too, Scooter. Night, Max." I was grateful he didn't say anything about the phone. Whew! I texted a quick goodnight to Harlan.

I picked up my clock to be sure the alarm was set—and noticed it had frozen at 7:20, the exact time of the electric light show. Normally, it would be flashing to remind me to reset it after a power outage. But it was frozen on the time instead. Yes! Photo evidence. I grabbed my phone and snapped a pic, before I reset the clock and set the alarm. Not much proof, but it was something. Harlan would believe me.

I closed my eyes, touched the butterfly at my neck, imagining Momma kissing me goodnight. A loneliness swept through me at the memory of something I missed more than walking. The gears in my brain whirled at a slower pace. Slower, slower, slower. What a long day. On the radio the DJ interrupted my music for an announcement: *Another robbery last night at . . .*

CHAPTER FIVE

The next morning, I snuggled Max while I inhaled one of my favorite smells—bacon. Uncle Ezra cooked bacon and pancakes every Saturday, rain or shine. Late summer sunshine already brightened my blue room, casting light on my collection of Star Wars figures. Momma, Daddy, and I had seen every movie so many times we could all quote our favorite lines.

My blinds had been raised, and my bathroom stuff set out for me before I woke. I didn't need Dad to do that anymore, but it meant so much to him to be able to help, so I never said anything. He always tried to find things to do to help me and got upset he couldn't do more.

Honestly, it did make it a little quicker to have everything where I needed it in the mornings. I wasn't much of a morning person, not before the accident, and not after.

Yoda smiled at me and I imagined him saying, "Good day, this will be." Whenever I needed help with a challenge, I considered myself a young Jedi at Yoda's feet, and tried to quote what his advice to me would be.

Momma once said, "That Yoda has more wisdom in his tiny body than most humans would have if they lived to be six hundred years old." He wasn't just a character in a movie to me—he was a link to Momma. I returned his smile and agreed that it would be a good day.

That bacon smell had started my day just right—my mouth watered, and Max scrambled out of the bed as soon as I moved my legs to the side. Early morning and late night in the bed, I was reminded how my legs didn't work the same as they had before the accident. Lying down made it easy to forget because my legs moved around fine then. It was only when I tried to stand and walk that they wouldn't work to hold me up, or not for very long anyway. It was hard to describe what it felt like, just not right, not strong.

The doctors said my spinal cord had been "insulted" in the accident. "We don't know how long it might last—maybe forever. We hope it's temporary." This morning I swallowed a twinge of the usual sadness and got ready to transfer to the Zoomster.

I pulled my pants on lying in bed, the easiest way to do that these days. Putting on pants in a wheelchair is not a great way to start a day! I had to lift myself so many times to keep from getting pressure sores that I didn't need any extra lifts in my day—even with my new strong-arm muscles. I missed skirts, but no way would I wear a skirt with legs that looked like sticks now. My arm muscles got bigger while my calf muscles disappeared.

I sat up to pull on my shirt. My blue t-shirt almost matched the sky out the window. Ready.

My wheelchair waited beside my bed. I flexed my new muscles, not weight-lifter arms, but much stronger arms than I used to have, and held onto the bed while I transferred to Zoomster. I could hold my weight standing for a minute now, after months of physical therapy. I stood still for as long as I could—like they taught me. I counted, trying to make it three minutes. I used the timer on my phone because three minutes stretched a lot longer than you'd think. The first time I did it on my own, I thought thirty seconds was three minutes.

Max waited for me to get settled in my chair before trotting into the bathroom ahead of me, used to our morning routine. Pee—that whole transfer thing again—and then brush teeth and splash water on my face. I'd slept in braids Gran put in so I didn't need to brush my hair. Done.

I headed to the kitchen. Max had a little extra swag in his wag too. Bacon, after all!

"Mornin' sunshine." Uncle Ezra flipped pancakes on the griddle as Max and I arrived in the room. Sun glinted on the bays of windows, dirtier than Momma ever allowed them to be.

Uncle Ezra looked so much like Dad I could barely tell them apart from fifty feet, but up close Uncle Ezra was a little thinner and had thicker hair—a huge point of jealousy with Dad. Uncle Ezra tormented Dad about it every chance he got. Uncle Ezra had movie star looks; Dad resembled the lead singer in a rock band after a two-hour set. They used to dress up on Halloween as Elvis and a rock star, and they still played the parts.

"What's cookin' good lookin'?" Uncle Ezra had the sunshine disposition of the family, according to Gran. Gran said Dad had been military material from birth—neat, respectful, and protective.

"Since it's Saturday, I expect you are." I smiled at his antics as he juggled eggs, then cracked them into a bowl with a flourish.

I rolled across the floor and set the table to Gran's standards, my regular job. Even though she went to quilting with her church ladies on Saturday mornings, standards are standards. I poured coffee for each of us and added the creams and sugars, with extras of each in my Yoda mug, which again reminded me I was a young Jedi, still learning the ropes. Maybe Zeb was my Yoda. How awesome! I shivered at the memory of the light show. Maybe I'd tell Uncle Ezra someday—he might get it.

I loved our huge yellow kitchen, where everything matched and no troubles from the outside world existed. Momma said a kitchen should be the heart of the home. Family meals had been a thing even before the accident took Momma away. And now they had become a way to honor her memory. It was the least we could do.

Blam, blam, blam! I jumped when the pounding at the front door suddenly echoed into the kitchen, bumping my elbow on my wheelchair. Max alerted us with his deep I-will-rip-your-leg-off bark. He's a pacifist, but woofs like a killer. Visitors seldom arrived in the morning around here, and those who did came in the back door for a cup of coffee in the kitchen. So, Max hadn't overreacted—the pounding startled us all.

The old door creaked as Dad opened it and mumbled a greeting. I wheeled to the kitchen doorway to check it out. A man stood at the door, a balding classmate of Dad's he met for beer every Friday afternoon at the only bar in town.

"Hey, Critter, what are you doing banging at the front door? You could've come in the usual way," Dad said.

"This here's official business. I need to ask you some questions," said Critter, a sheriff's deputy, in his khaki uniform, his shortish figure dwarfed by the opening. He'd been nicknamed Critter as a kid after some grown-up remarked what a tiny little critter he was. Nicknames tended to stick in these parts. Pretty near everybody has a nickname in the hills.

He wore his official business voice today, along with his freshly pressed uniform, and he'd used the front door instead of the back. He looked as nervous as a cat in a room full of rocking chairs. I frowned, my gaze darting back and forth between the two of them. My heart was in my throat. Had Gran been in an accident?

"Sure, Critter, whatever." Dad walked over and sat on the edge of the sofa. Critter followed. Dad motioned for me to get his coffee. I think he wanted to get me out of there, but I pretended I didn't know what he meant, and stayed right in that doorway, in case Critter had bad news to deliver. Uncle Ezra glided past me with some coffee for Dad, but when he wasn't invited to linger, he returned to the kitchen. Not about Gran then, or Critter would've talked to both of them. I sighed in relief.

"Have you had any strange visitors to the paintball fields lately? Noticed anything unusual about anyone? Anyone at all?" Critter's notebook stood ready; pen poised to record important information. Everything about him screamed deputy-on-duty this morning, even though I knew for a fact that the most serious business he usually had involved old Mr. Grady letting his cows roam out into the neighbor's pastures.

Critter didn't need to be too harsh to deal with cow tippers or folks who ran the few stop signs around here anyway. Still, we all knew he was a serious-as-heck lawman when he needed to be. His 5'6" frame could look 6' tall when he stopped a teenager for speeding. That could end up a come-to-Jesus moment real quick if they gave any backtalk.

"Nope. Just our regulars, the teenagers, our usual team-building parties, and military types." Dad relaxed into the overstuffed sofa, took a sip of his coffee, and winked at me. "Want some coffee, Critter?"

"This here's serious, now. And, yeah, cream and sugar, Scooter." Critter smiled at me, then frowned at Dad, then smiled at me again. I got dizzy watching. "I wouldn't mind some of that bacon I smell either."

"Sure thing, Deputy, sir." I saluted Critter and stayed just inside the kitchen doorway listening to the conversation I wasn't supposed to hear.

"I need to warn you about this here robber that's makin' the rounds. He seems like he's making his way over to our neck of the woods. He just hit the Dairy Del and Mr. Hogan's little grocery over in the next holler. Seems like he knows how to get in, get out right quick, and not get caught. He could hit you on a weekend. You have a few dollars pass through there, on a busy Saturday especially." Critter glanced at me. "You know, I'd hate to see anything set you back with the business."

Dad glared at Critter. Red rose up Critter's neck, and he exchanged a look with Dad I didn't understand.

Critter closed up his notebook without a word written in it, a disappointed look on his face. Guess he'd hoped Dad might've noticed something unusual. Guess that's how an investigation goes at first—lots of questions, not many answers. I'd never seen inside a robbery investigation before. This could be fun, as long as they didn't come for us.

Dad narrowed his eyes at me and waved his hand. I could take a hint. Time for me to leave.

"I can take care of myself," Dad said as I left. He didn't need to explain. Critter knew Dad would take care of us out here, whatever it took. Critter also knew Dad might stretch it a little if someone acted the fool. He'd turn a hose on teenagers making trouble to scare the pants off them. Dad believed in peace, just like Yoda, but had said more than once that he'd defend his family the same way he had defended his country—however he was called on to do it.

I got busy on the coffee and a plate of bacon for Critter, so Uncle Ezra could deliver it. He kept glancing to the doorway, clearly dying to join the conversation. The food delivery would give him an excuse to find out what was going on. Critter didn't linger too much longer, although he just about licked his plate clean and had a second cup of coffee before he took off to sound the alarm around town, our local Paul Revere. I didn't hear the rest of the conversation, but my ears itched like crazy while I did some kitchen chores. Were they socializing or was he giving Dad more warnings now that I was out of the room?

At one point "Your mother might have …" drifted in, and I dared to stop the running dishwasher and listen hard. Nothing more about Gran. Maybe Critter had asked how she was doing. I didn't think too much about it at the time. Maybe I should have.

After Critter left, Dad went to get ready for the day, while Uncle Ezra came to finish up in the kitchen, like any master chef worthy of his name would do. I'd found plenty of jobs I could still do, but my kitchen duty was over.

Weird to have robberies in our neck of the woods. No way any robber would get *our* money without a fight. Critter hadn't said how many robberies there'd been, but I could find out. I'd corner Uncle Ezra later and find out all the details. Dad told him everything, and he'd love spilling the beans to me and Gran. Even if Dad didn't tell him the scoop, small towns are full of gossip, and I was a good listener. I liked to be in the know about things around here after all.

CHAPTER SIX

Harlan bounced through the back door at nine. Harlan bounced everywhere. His enthusiasm for all things in the universe—and all things supernatural—made me love him. Marvel heroes splashed across the front of his t-shirt, and his untamed black curls were fresh from the shower, still glistening with the water sitting on top of his 'do, what he called his loc fade.

He was the same as when I'd first met him, only taller, way taller. I'd been in Kindergarten, crying because I was lost. His first-grade smartness impressed me, and when he delivered me to my classroom and Mrs. Duck, I vowed to trust him forever. He's been the best friend a girl could have ever since! He needed a sister, and I needed a big brother—one of those destiny things.

He tucked right into his waiting breakfast, one of the perks of his job at the paintball field. "Are these bacon-flavored pancakes? Who invented that?" Harlan smiled at me, and quickly wolfed down a huge stack. Clearly, that flavor combination worked for him.

By now our two-year age difference showed up in our sizes. Even though we were only one grade apart because of the way our birthdays fell, his head start was beginning to give him a height advantage. Mine was harder to tell from the chair, but I hadn't shot up like him yet. He had started middle school last year, and I'd be going soon, but in a different hallway. That change had been hard after all our years in the same school.

I craned my neck harder to see his face—it took a little more effort now, and I got a crick in my neck if he didn't come down to my chair level sometimes. No stubble today. He'd recently shaved for the first time and had been quite proud of it. I didn't want him to be looking like a man already. I couldn't stand it if some girl came along and snatched my best friend away. I hated to admit it, but he'd make a great boyfriend for someone—not yet though.

"Got the idea from Rachael Ray off the Food Network." Uncle Ezra's face beamed as he finished up the dishes. "Well, not exactly, but I started with her idea. Glad *somebody* liked them." He gave me the side-eye, and called Max a good dog, clearly not pleased that I'd eaten a bowl of cereal instead of his pancakes this morning.

"You can fix these for me any time." Harlan showed his appreciation by finishing his second Paul Bunyan stack, drowned in maple syrup, in less time than it takes to skin a squirrel.

"A growing boy can't have too many pancakes." Uncle Ezra spoke like that was one of his hill country commandments. Harlan's huge appetite for his cooking always had him grinning like a possum. I don't think anybody ever cooked at Harlan's house. He'd asked Uncle Ezra to give him cooking lessons. And he'd never missed having a meal with us when invited.

"Arm wrestle for folding vests today," I challenged Harlan. Since all my therapy and butt lifts in the chair to relieve pressure, I'd become the arm-wrestling queen. And I hated to fold the vests. It was like making your bed—you were just gonna mess it up again.

"You're on. I started lifting some weights. This is embarrassing. You're two years younger than me."

"Best out of five." I got in position.

Five times we both struggled. I'd been stomping him. But we hadn't wrestled for a while. He *had* been working out. He won three to two. And didn't gloat too much. Hush my mouth if he hadn't passed me up in something else.

Harlan and I had a few minutes before we needed to head over to work, so we excused ourselves and filmed a quick video post to add to the video I made right after Zeb's visit. He recorded quickly—we'd edit and post later today.

Hi, everybody, it's Scooter and Harlan, sharing some exciting news about a post coming soon. I've been told all my life that our property is haunted, and I believe I know at least one of the spirits who visits, my great-, great-, great-grandfather who served in the Civil War, and is buried on our land. See the link in the comments to read more about Zebediah. It was said that he frequently came back in spirit to visit the eight children he left behind. I believe it's true, and I think Zeb wants to talk. We've included the video I made right after a visit from him in my room. It was scary and awesome at the same time. You'll see. I'd like to find video proof of Zeb, and we'll take you along while we try. More coming soon! Be sure to like, subscribe, turn on notifications, comment, and share. You know we love to hear from you, so tell us about your favorite haunted properties. Bye, now. See you next week, same time, same channel for our (I paused, and Harlan popped in the screen) presentation from your favorite ghost hunters.

It took a little longer than I expected. Just as I prepared to pull my new camera out from under the bed to show Harlan, Uncle Ezra called, "Let's get a move on, kids."

Harlan and I hurried back to the kitchen. Dad arrived, in khaki pants and collared shirt, ready for the business day. He took Saturdays very seriously, our bread and butter day, he said. "Morning, Harlan. Everybody ready to head over? Paintball awaits!"

CHAPTER SEVEN

I couldn't wait until Dad and Uncle Ezra got far enough in front of us for our voices not to be heard. They led the way to the office, half a football field away from the house. Dad did most of the talking, probably filling Uncle Ezra in on Critter's warnings.

I kept Zoomster on low speed so Harlan and I could take our time on the asphalt path. Harlan waited until they were out of hearing before asking about last night. "Do you think old Zeb will come back?"

"I don't know. Maybe he can only come on his birthday." I shrugged. "Not like we can go buy spirit bait at the grocery. And he's never come inside the house before, at least not that there's any record of."

"We have to get to the cemetery. Try to talk to him." Harlan wanted to meet a ghost as much as I did. He had to be a little jealous that I had all the fun. Actually, it had been as scary as could be at first. Only after it was all over did I get excited.

"Maybe tomorrow." I had an idea, but we'd need more time to plan it than we'd likely have today. "I want to set up a camera. In our cemetery. Motion-activated." Maybe a sneak attack was the only way we'd ever catch a ghost on film—most ghost hunters believed that ghosts were camera-shy. And I planned to catch one sooner or later, hopefully sooner, and I'd love for it to be Zeb. Mostly, I wanted to catch Momma's spirit, but she didn't seem ready yet, so Zeb would be a great catch for now. At least connecting with a family spirit who might know Momma could fill some of this emptiness in my heart. While waiting on Momma I'd stay busy learning how to communicate better with spirits.

"And where are we gonna get that kind of camera?" Harlan's voice verged on sarcastic.

Easy does it—no need to go too fast with the surprise. "I found one online." Dad gave Harlan and me a small paycheck for our work. Harlan bought clothes and groceries, but I saved most of what I earned. So, I *deserved* to have the best ghost hunting equipment available. After all, I'd worked for that money.

"Won't you get in trouble with your dad if you get one?" Harlan had seen Dad mad a few times. When Dad puffed up in his military stance, no one crossed him, not even Uncle Ezra or Gran. And Harlan practically worshipped Dad, who'd been good to him since the day he met him at the school play, when I'd been Ariel and he'd been the cutest seahorse ever seen in our holler.

"How else are we ever gonna find Momma? Or see a spirit? Besides, it's my money. Anyway, I already ordered it." The last I added in an undertone, half hoping he wouldn't hear. I evaded his question about Dad, since I was counting on Dad never finding out what I'd done. "And it's in my bedroom, under my bed." I glanced at Harlan in time to catch his glare at me. He'd heard.

"Don't you think we should've decided that together? You know I don't have any extra money." His voice hitched a little, a sure sign he was really upset with me.

Wow! Not the reaction I'd expected. Except maybe I had expected it but decided to take my chances. Reckon that's part of why I wanted him to open it with me, so he'd "own" it too.

"Sorry. Thought you'd be excited." Maybe he needed time to think about it. He looked like a cat getting baptized.

"I thought we were a team." He kicked a rock beside the path. Max skittered after it. "That's – not – how – teams – work." He emphasized each word.

The paintball building suddenly loomed in front of us. He'd taken it way worse than I expected. Mostly, he seemed more worried about Dad. But also about being left out.

We *needed* this camera. Spirits got nervous when humans were around, and often hid themselves. It might be different if we weren't standing there holding a camera. Besides, we couldn't be down at the cemetery all the time, but a mounted camera could film when we weren't there. Spirits usually came out in the dark. Momma's year was almost over—we didn't have time to waste.

I hadn't had time to ask Uncle Ezra what he knew about the robberies, with the camera distraction and all. The spirits were much more interesting to think about than that robber.

At the doors, I got ready to switch gears. Paintball customers were a fun crowd, and Saturdays always flew. Maybe I'd hear more gossip about the robberies today anyway. Wonder if Dad would pay attention to Critter's warnings to be careful.

8

CHAPTER EIGHT

Max and I followed Harlan into the storefront—the most fun business in town. We'd work for free, but we never told Dad that. The money was nice.

Thanks to my ancestors I'd never have to drive twenty miles to work. Walking, or in my case hitching a ride in Zoomster, from your house to your business was a luxury. Lots of thanks to Zebediah, the first ancestor who bought all these acres so many years ago, and thanks to all the others who'd managed to hold on to most of the acreage over the years. Hope Dad could keep it going—he'd hate losing Momma's investment even more than losing our family property.

Outside, the property stretched for acres in every direction—woods, fields, streams, abandoned buildings, the big bus, and some junked cars—enough to give paintball players plenty of cover when hiding. The customers were mostly neighbors or regulars, and close with all of us who worked here, and everyone (mostly anyway) was really nice.

Harlan's brows still furrowed whenever he glanced my way. He barely said anything. I wouldn't have been surprised to see smoke coming out of his ears. He hadn't been this mad at me in a while—maybe ever.

Harlan and I entered the space that held the paint, vests, visors, and guns, with Max tangling around our legs in the cramped room. Zoomster took up a lot of space—it had been easier back here when my legs worked. Lots of things had been easier when my legs worked. I prayed they'd work again someday.

"What a mess!" I thought we'd done a better job of cleaning up last time.

"You were the one in a big hurry last time!"

Harlan snapped. He tripped over Max, caught himself on the arm of Zoomster and nearly tipped all three of us over.

That broke the ice!

We nearly split our sides laughing until Dad said, "Are you guys ready to open?"

No, no we weren't.

"Sure, we're ready." Harlan signaled me to shush and got busy organizing our mess. He quickly sorted equipment into the right bins and moved a selection of the things I'd need to the front counter. This tag team approach was the only way we could operate in the small space—me at the window and Harlan being my legs.

I didn't miss Momma quite so much when we were busy here because she never used to come over to the shop or fields, so it wasn't like the kitchen, or my bedroom, where I still see her everywhere. Her commitment to the family business didn't stretch quite far enough to make her keep company with grown men shooting paint every Saturday, she said. It *had* stretched far enough though to hand over all of her savings to Dad so he could hang on to the family business, in danger of closing when they married. She loved Dad—paintball, not so much.

Usually I enjoyed our long Saturdays and most of our customers. Harlan and I didn't have to fool with any annoying people. Uncle Ezra either cheered them up, or Dad threw them out like old grease.

I slid the tip jar in front of the window, but my mind wandered to the cemetery. Time to get that camera up.

I put a smile on my face and in my voice. Like Gran said, you can't ever be too polite, but it's easy to slip over and be rude. Rude didn't earn any tips, but super-sweet smiles did. By the end of every day, we had a jar full of green—mostly ones, but ones add up. Between the salary Dad paid us and the tips, we raked it in on Saturdays.

Dad wandered over to inspect our station. Harlan by then had it ready to go.

"When Ezra and I go out on the field today, you guys lock up," Dad said. "Just in case."

So, he *was* paying attention to the warnings. Generally, we only locked up when we left for the day.

"Yes, sir," Harlan answered. He'd be sure to do it too.

Outside, a car honked and brakes squealed.

Time to get busy. I focused on the work ahead of me. I didn't mind leaving behind those thoughts about needing to lock doors.

Ford trucks and souped-up cars piled helter-skelter into our gravel parking lot. I loved that sound—trucks crunching the gravel and the parking lot filling up. The temperature had registered a perfect 68 degrees on our giant Coca-Cola thermostat that decorated the barn on our way over.

Paintballers loved weather like today—just cool enough to make the camouflage clothes bearable, but warm enough to make you suffer and sweat a little, mimicking a tiny part of what they imagined war to be like. Surprisingly, even though Dad had served in a war, it didn't offend him to see people do pretend battle. He said that kids started playing soldier as soon as they started talking, and this was a grown-up version of child's play. A harmless way to fill a day.

The first slam of the door was followed by voices filling the space. The store was big, and people spread out, shopping and chattering. But most of them lined up at our counter for paintballs and equipment.

Lots of the people in line were all decked out

in camo and their own paint gun belts—serious about winning the paint battles, and they didn't want to be kept waiting for supplies.

"Did you order this perfect weather?" a regular smiled and took his equipment.

"I brought my son today. Time he learned how to duck some paint," another regular said, pointing out his son as he ordered double of everything.

"Twenty dollars," Harlan and I repeated many times as we worked our counter, accepting the standard payment for equipment and an allotment of paint. The special platform Uncle Ezra made put me on a perfect level with the counter.

Harlan grabbed the equipment from the racks, and I took the money and passed their stuff over. I stuffed twenty after twenty in the money pouch on the side of my chair. It grew thick as people paid for the tiny balls of paint. I wondered for the first time ever about a robber coming in while I had a pouch full of money. The robber could even be someone we'd seen here, someone who had bought paint from us today. That was the scary part—no one knew who the robber was or when or where he might strike again.

I took a deep breath. The worst of the rush was over, although players would still arrive for a while. The almost empty room echoed now as Dad and Uncle Ezra exchanged a few words.

Then out of nowhere a guy slapped down a twenty and said, "Heard you'll be in classes with my nephew over at the middle school. Name of Trevor." My skin crawled. The guy we called Creepy Pete had snuck up on us again.

"Oh," I managed to mutter, as I floundered for a polite answer and my smile. I'd been trying to forget that I'd be starting at a new school soon. Creepy Pete seldom strung so many words together.

The only thing good about leaving elementary school was being in the same school building as Harlan again. But Pete had more words today.

"He says he knows who you are," Pete said, not unkindly. His lips twitched into what must be his best smile.

I nodded and returned his smile before Pete hurried off with his paint. We called this regular Creepy Pete because he appeared out of nowhere, spoke very little and unexpectedly, and disappeared as quickly as he appeared. The only word to describe that was creepy—well, maybe sneaky would work, but he didn't seem to sneak, just appear, creepy like.

Harlan shook his head. "His nephew, Trevor, is a really nice kid. Maybe we're wrong about old Creepy. Maybe he's shy or something."

"How does he do that? Appear out of thin air. Like a ghost?" I tucked Pete's twenty into my bulging pouch of money.

Then we got busy again selling paint to the last wave of customers and forgot about Creepy Pete.

The contest we'd advertised seemed to have more than our usual number still trickling in. Dad would award prizes, free equipment for their next game to the lucky winners today at the O.K. Corral—the most popular field with the players.

I liked paintball. This was only pretend battle, not like Mixed Martial Arts or boxing where people hit to hurt. Paintballs did sting if they hit just right, and you could get some pretty nasty welts and sometimes torn skin if you were too close to someone. But mostly people didn't get hurt.

The players had fun, got lost in pretend for a while to get away from their worries. If you didn't get away from your worries once in a while, you might get overly sad about what life threw in your path, so I was all for some fun myself. *My* fun was ghost hunting, like Momma. And playing the guitar. And watching Star Wars movies.

One regular arrived head to toe in camouflage with his huge custom paint belt. "Fill me up," he said as he slapped down four twenty-dollar bills, same as every week he didn't have overtime down in the mines. He puffed up his chest and marched away. "Nice to get out in that sunshine." Must be awful to be down in those mines like he was every day. Uncle Ezra said going down in those mines that much, smack dab in coal land, scissored a man's soul into a different shape.

Dad approached our window with a smile. "A thousand in equipment this morning," he spoke in an undertone. People would pay a fortune for just the right face shield, or paint belt, or camouflage, and we were always getting newer and better styles in. "Word's getting out about the hunting gear and t-shirts. Guy came all the way from North Carolina." Dad had said if he was going to run this business, he was going to be the best around. He constantly made improvements to the store and the games, which is what kept people coming back. But it also left Dad worrying a lot about money, it seemed.

"Scooter, I need your cash." Dad held out his hand.

I handed over a wad of mostly twenties I hadn't counted yet. We never counted if a single customer was around, something about that being rude to do. Uncle Ezra had some song he'd bust into about not countin' your money while you're sittin' at the table.

Dad never left much money in the store. He always said there was no point in everybody seeing how much money we took in—it was none of their darn business. Money business was private business in the hills—stiff-necked pride kept being poor a secret. He carried away the cash he'd collected that day, his footsteps loud in the quiet. Max followed. How did Max know to do that? He'd done that since I started working here, like he had a sixth sense that Dad needed a guard.

Uncle Ezra rang up another sale at the cash register for a late arrival, a guy I'd never seen before. So tall that he hovered over Uncle Ezra, who was tall himself. The stranger's hair was so white that it made me think of a panda for some reason, maybe his round face. Panda's gaze followed Dad out the door. Like he knew Dad was leaving with money.

"Did you see that?" I asked Harlan.

"What?"

"How that guy watched Dad leave with the money."

Harlan's only answer was a roll of his eyes. Now I was being paranoid, thinking everybody was a robber.

I didn't know where Dad went when he left like that. Critter's warning that morning replayed in my memory. Dad had always been really careful about the money—it disappeared from the storefront, sometimes without being counted once he saw it piling up on busy days. A robber would never find it in this building because it didn't stay very long. But who knew where it went, or if Dad was safe getting it there? Max would at least scare some people off with his you-could-be-my-next-meal bark if he needed to. I trusted Max to keep Dad safe.

9

CHAPTER NINE

I held my breath a little bit until Dad came back in the store. All of the robberies around town must've put my imagination into overdrive. To be safe I moved the money pouch to the other side of my chair. I'd added more money in the pouch since the merchandise store closed, so I had money Dad hadn't collected yet.

Men and boys, a few girls, and our star woman player, nicknamed Champ, still huddled in the staging area, getting their directions from Uncle Ezra. "Keep a safe distance from each other unless you want a bruise the size of a watermelon. *Duck* and *run* are your friends on the field." Uncle Ezra loved to ham it up with our visitors, and Dad gladly turned over that job to him. Except for the very end, when Dad gave the BIG WARNINGS about safety. It was all fun and games with Uncle Ezra, but for Dad it was his world.

Harlan and I played our usual game while we listened, guessing the time it would take for the switch from laughter to quiet. It usually took the crowd between ten seconds and a minute to quiet down once Uncle Ezra turned it over to Dad.

"Forty-five seconds today. That guy with the ponytail is gonna be a problem." Harlan picked the exact time I'd been thinking.

"Forty seconds." I got ready to start the stopwatch.

Harlan won our contest; it took almost exactly forty-five seconds for the crowd to settle down. Ponytail guy missed Dad's stern cue to listen up and almost got thrown out.

People always pushed and shoved, in a civilized Southern way of course, to be first on the field and stake out a good position. Some people liked specific places or games on the compound, especially what we called the O.K. Corral. That's where we organized two teams against each other, gave 'em a few rules and turned 'em loose in an area with decaying buildings and that old school bus, opposite our little fenced-in cemetery.

I didn't usually mind staying behind at the store, but today I'd love to see the battle at the Corral.

"Masks on," Dad gave a final reminder for newbies.

Uncle Ezra opened the gates with great drama to release the players onto the field. He fired up their four-wheeler, ready for the corral challenge. Dad and Uncle Ezra would ride the four-wheeler and keep an eye on things.

Once in a while, some teenagers shot someone from super close range, and needed a little help. They ended up with welts and bruises when they did something stupid like that, but we'd never had to send anyone to the emergency room. If they did it on purpose, Dad sent them home with a warning. But twice, and he'd ban them. Sometimes someone twisted an ankle in the woodsy terrain and needed a ride back to base. The four-wheeler came in handy for those emergencies.

Harlan and I had never minded them being out all day since we caught up with plans for our channel during the down time and didn't really want to be out there with all that paint flying. We spent enough time fighting paint chips everywhere. Harlan had even invented wheel covers for my chair that we only used here so Zoomster didn't track paint all over the house.

I'd never thought much about us being alone in the storefront until today, after Critter's visit, and the stuff on the radio about the robberies. Harlan would protect me, if he could, and Max would too. But what would two kids and a dog do against a serious robber? I needed to learn more about those robberies. Maybe I needed to brush up on self-defense. Or at least figure out where to hide the money.

Once the warriors emptied the staging area and poured onto the field, I let out a sigh of relief. Time to chill. With so much swagger charging up the room this morning over the competition, I had barely caught a breath between customers. Lots of these guys were going to be eating their braggy words soon. At the same time, a tiny worry tickled the back of my mind—a tiny worry about that robber. No matter how many times it got shoved to the back, it scuttled back out like a sand crab, a little bit sideways but still there. Our peaceful little town wasn't prepared for bad stuff. I stuffed the worry down. Harlan and I had a lot to discuss.

I rolled out of the confined space. Harlan stayed behind to organize the chaos. He could organize faster without tripping over me and Max.

Just then, the outer door slammed closed. I almost jumped out of my wheelchair.

A regular, Walter, hovered in the office doorway with a stupid grin on his face, outfitted in his camo as usual. Why did he always have to be late? He was never on time to join a group like most people were. He stood only a few feet away from me since I was out from behind the counter already. His eyes locked on the money pouch on the side of my wheelchair, now pretty empty. He pulled his eyes away at last and replaced his startled look with his regular grin.

"What's up, ghost girl?" He knuckled my hair and punched my shoulder. I hid my grimace by ducking my head. I wasn't one of the guys and didn't care for this up-close contact like I was an old buddy of his. "Any new spirits in your world?" Ever since I'd made the mistake of answering his question about what I enjoyed in my spare time with information about our YouTube channel, I'd been "ghost girl," a nickname I wouldn't mind if he didn't add that short edge to his tone when he said it, like he thought it was the funniest thing ever for a kid to believe in spirits.

"Not much going on. Big crowd's already out there." I nodded toward the exit to the fields, separate from the front door he'd just come through, hoping he'd take the hint. Harlan and I needed to talk. Some days players trickled back in almost as soon as the last ones went out, but we usually had at least a little while to ourselves.

"On my way, on my way." Walter threw an extra twenty dollars in with the money for his admission and paint, grabbed his goggles, vest, and paint, and called back over his shoulder to Harlan as he stomped out, "Get you and Scooter some pop and have one waiting for me when I come in." No "please" ever came with his twenties. Gran would not approve. I bet he thanked grown-ups. "Please" and "thank you" were holler commandments.

"Yes, sir." Harlan put the pop money in his pocket and raised an eyebrow in my direction. Walter was the only customer who tipped so much, and the only one who went out of his way every week to talk to us. We appreciated how friendly he was, even if he annoyed us with his late arrival and sometimes stupid remarks. His twenty-dollar tips almost made up for his lack of manners. I couldn't make up my mind if I liked him or not. The ghost girl greeting rubbed me the wrong way.

Walter didn't fit the usual type of players we got here. He threw a lot of money around to play. He didn't play in a group, or do any of the competitions, or hang around like the other players did. He kept mostly to himself. He sort of stuck out like a mule in a herd of cows. Come to think of it, he hadn't been coming that long, and Critter asked about new people. Why did Walter even come to the fields? Was he a wannabe soldier? Oh, well, it was his money. Hopefully.

CHAPTER TEN

Harlan and I finally had a chance to talk about what had happened last night. We'd been dying to talk about what Zeb's visit might mean.

"I wonder if his grave will look any different. Like maybe his spirit disturbed it," Harlan said during a quiet moment.

I hadn't thought about that. "Maybe. But I don't think so, or cemeteries might look messed up all the time."

"If they weren't having the big contest today, I could run down there real quick and check it out."

"No way you're going without me." I might've sounded a little mad because he side-eyed me. I couldn't believe he even said that!

"It's not like *you* could sneak down there," he said and cracked me up with his imitation of me wheeling in a hurry, setting the gears on Zoomster. I could get there okay, but not sneak. All over our property were paths Zoomster could navigate. Paintball's property had once been a hospital for patients with tuberculosis, and the paths had given them places where they could get out of the cramped, overcrowded hospital. Many had needed to be rolled in wooden wheelchairs, specially made for them. It was almost like the property had been special ordered for me, but our family had owned it for so many years, long before the government built the hospital on part of the property, loaned to them for that crisis. They'd paved paths that had already been in place for as far back as we had photos of things around here. Maybe time was some kind of continuum we didn't understand yet, like spirits, and my ancestors sensed I'd be needing paths someday.

I had to laugh at his imitation of me being sneaky.

"You bought a camera without me,

remember?" He pinned his gaze on me. I rolled my eyes and rolled away.

Visiting the cemetery would have to wait until a Sunday, when the business closed so everybody could go to church. In a town like ours, tradition won out over a business like ours. We could be open, but without enough business to make any money. It wasn't worth the effort. Besides, we were a church-going family. Always had been. Momma saw God as the coordinator of all our spirits—living and dead.

Even though I tried to explain the astonishing light show of Zeb's visit in full living color to Harlan as we worked to restore order in the equipment rental room and the store, it was like explaining the ocean to someone who'd never seen it. Harlan sometimes said that maybe I had a gift he didn't have that made communicating with spirits easier for me. Maybe he was right. I felt something deep inside me that wanted to talk with spirits, even before Momma died. Maybe because she'd talked about it all my life.

It's been proven that some people have better psychic powers than others. Just like we can't explain why some genius kid can play Beethoven perfectly at the age of five, maybe we can't explain why some people pick up signals from spirits better than others. That's a gift that would be wonderful to have—the talking to spirits, not the piano thing. I'd rather play guitar, like Dad.

Maybe I was a "sensitive," and I suspected Max was too. That's probably why he was the perfect dog for me—connected by our ability to sense spirits.

I pulled out my phone and called back over my shoulder, "Watch the door to make sure no one comes in. I have to answer Undead1998, the one who claims Momma's video catching that orb at St. Louis cemetery wasn't real. They're at it again."

"I forgot what your dad said! I promised to lock it!" He rushed to flip the lock to fix his mistake, but before he could Gran opened it. So much for keeping people locked out today.

"What are you doing here?" I asked. It was like seeing a swordfish in a fishbowl. I smiled so she'd know I was curious, not being impertinent, one of her favorite words and least favorite behaviors. Seems like I was sometimes without knowing it.

"I noticed your iPad on the kitchen table. I

thought you used it on Saturdays." She smiled, not at all like a swordfish. When she looked all around the storefront, frown lines furrowed above her eyes.

Gran came to the side of my wheelchair and plopped her huge carryall in my lap. She dug around and came up with my iPad, but not before I saw the wad of hundred-dollar bills she shoved to the bottom of the bag.

I swallowed my gum. What in the name of heaven was Gran doing with all that money?

"Thanks." I tried to see more inside her bag, but Gran snatched it away like my lap was on fire.

"How was business this morning? Better?"

Gran never asked about paintball. What did she know that I didn't know anyway?

"Business was fine today. Why?"

Gran ignored my question. She gave us both a hug and skedaddled out of there. My brain twirled like a kaleidoscope as the door slammed behind her. Harlan rushed behind her to lock the door. What a strange visit.

"Did you see what I saw?" I asked even though he was probably too far away to see.

"Your Gran's new bag?" Harlan asked.

Tell him or not? He'd been so mad about the camera, but this was Gran. She was his Gran too. "Gran had a wad of hundred-dollar bills in her purse." I rushed the words to get them out of my mouth, like spitting out poison.

"Wait. What? Maybe she'd been to the bank."

"No. A wad." I showed how thick the wad had been with my hands. Harlan rolled his eyes.

"There's an explanation, Scooter. Don't be jumping to conclusions."

I sulked for a few minutes while Harlan ran to answer the store phone. Gran probably was carrying the restaurant money around for some strange reason. Maybe she was getting forgetful. I'd better be watching out for her. It bothered me that she had all that money with a robber running around. Could she be . . . ? No, Gran would never do that. Not ever. Not for anything. Not even if her restaurant was going to close. Not even if Dad was getting ready to lose the paintball fields? Maybe she'd noticed how careful Dad had gotten with money. And she knew about all the medical bills. Hmmm.

Harlan patted my shoulder when he came back from the phone. The iPad in my lap reminded me why I'd pulled out my phone.

I posted a quick response on the blog while Harlan stood guard. Since we were on the clock, we didn't usually pull out our phones, but I needed to answer that one. I *wanted* to answer that one.

The afternoon dragged. A short distance away our family spirit waited for a visit from us, and we couldn't go—not that we'd want to be there right now. No self-respecting spirit was likely to appear during a paintball battle. The O.K. Corral near the cemetery would be rocking with paint flying from all directions.

It might have been fun to watch that from a safe distance, like on the old school bus out there, but we weren't allowed on that anymore, since the wheelchair lift had gotten a little fussy. The day I'd gotten stuck on the bus, it had taken a while to get me off. Not so much me—they just lifted me off. But old Zoomster had been a little more trouble. Before that had happened, Harlan and I hung out there a lot, our version of a treehouse.

Finally, the crowds staggered back in from the fields and returned equipment. They took their time, slapped high fives like we wanted to hang around forever. Stood in clusters of two or three and rehashed their bravery. You'd think we offered a prize for the last person to turn in their equipment. Most weekend warriors didn't fall into the hurry-home-to-my-Saturday-date type. More likely, they'd continue their gaming talk over a few beers up at the bar. Only the guys and girls in their teens left early—maybe they had more to look forward to, or maybe they got bored faster, or ran out of money and paint, more likely.

Walter, last to arrive, staggered in late from the fields. "What's up, guys?" He slammed his equipment down.

"How'd you avoid the battle out there?" Harlan handed Walter his pop.

"It got a little too crazy out there today, so I hid out behind that big bus." Walter had not a speck of paint on him. How was that possible?

At last, the door shut behind the last customer, and the long workday ended. Dad had mentioned pizza earlier, but I reckoned he'd be too worn out from this long day. I'd sure love to have some pizza. And Gran should be there—she usually was on her busy night. Maybe she'd mention the money.

CHAPTER ELEVEN

W ho's up for pizza?" Dad asked as he locked the door, with a clink from his huge chain that must've held fifty keys. "Gran would love to feed us."

Dad and Uncle Ezra had already changed clothes and shoes, leaving behind the paint chips that wanted to cling to everything they touched. Harlan had stored my wheel covers, which kept Zoomster clean while we worked.

"My treat," said Uncle Ezra. Easy enough to say since Gran had never let us pay for a single thing at her restaurant.

My stomach demanded attention—like Max whining for a treat—feed me, please feed me. My morning cereal had long since left me hungry. On Saturdays we snacked when we could, if we could. There was never time to eat lunch on a busy Saturday. Cheetos and a Snickers, fave foods, took the edge off the hunger but they weren't really sticking to my ribs. Gran would not approve. A Southern gran with hungry kids was worse than a lemon pie with no meringue.

She stayed busy all day Saturday with her church friends, her "beauty" appointment, and her busiest night of the week at the restaurant. That left Saturday the one day of the week we fended for ourselves, from Uncle Ezra's morning pancakes to dinner out or burgers on the grill, or once in a while a special concoction from Uncle Ezra for dinner. Most of his concoctions turned out great, but Saturdays as busy as today at paintball didn't allow any time for him to visit the kitchen during the day and whip up dinner, much to his disappointment.

"Do I get to go?" Harlan swung Max-like eyes at Dad, not really necessary since he always went with us, but a little attention to Dad never hurt, and Harlan had wonderful manners, according to Gran. He also never took anything for granted the way I sometimes did.

Harlan didn't talk much about his family, but spent as much time as possible with mine, and I sensed, in the way best friends can, that things might not be so great at home. Harlan's uncle dropped him off and picked him up a lot of the time, and he showed up for Harlan, but beyond that we knew little. I never pried. Almost never, I should say. Small towns gossip, and there was gossip about Harlan's daddy.

"Not tonight . . ." Dad started, but his grin took over and he couldn't finish. He punched Harlan on the shoulder and said, "Just kidding. Pile in. Great job with the mad rush at the end. I hate when everybody leaves at the exact same time. But they always seem to, especially on a competition day."

"We haven't been to the restaurant for a while. Gran will be tickled as a chipmunk in a peanut factory to see us." Uncle Ezra laughed out loud and repeated, "A chipmunk full of peanuts."

I hated all the trouble it now took to load me and the wheelchair, but a trip to the restaurant, called Rosie's, was totally worth it. When Momma died, we'd lived on Gran's restaurant food and casseroles from neighbors until Uncle

Ezra arrived to help us. Dad stayed busy with my therapy appointments and keeping the business going at first. But his missing Momma seemed to crash at him like a tsunami all the time and kept him a little absentminded about meals and stuff.

Dad and Uncle Ezra grew up eating Gran's pizza of course. They loved her *slightly* more than her pizza, but it was a close call. Guess all that time in the restaurant kitchen gave Uncle Ezra his itch to cook, and it didn't surface until he had to cook for us.

We piled into our specially designed, paint-splashed van and headed to the center of town, the quietest little Main Street in all of Kentucky. Rosie's Pizza and Hoagie Shop, here we come.

Our van rocked. Instead of a boring, ordinary wheelchair van, we had turned ours into a rolling advertisement, splashed full of red, white, and blue paint splatters. Dad chose the red, white, and blue theme in honor of the good old U. S. of A., like that song he loved.

We parked close by and piled into the busy restaurant. The loud chatter hurt my ears. But the smell! Nothing in the world smelled better than pizza baking in the old brick ovens. Home, safety, food, and warmth curled from the ovens.

Usually Gran bustled around the restaurant like the town mayor, table hopping and checking on everybody. People would be disappointed if Gran didn't visit with them a minute. Tonight, she sat at a corner table with Critter, heads nearly touching, brows furrowed. As soon as they saw us, it was like a curtain got pulled on their worried faces. What in the world was going on?

I rolled toward the table and overheard "he's questioning her about the robberies" from a table I passed. When I turned to look, the guy talking was the one I called Panda, from paintball— the new guy with white hair who'd watched Dad so close when he left with the money. I'd checked out his name on the sign-in sheet. Nick. Harlan had thought I was being paranoid when I mentioned it. But I'd never seen him at paintball and never seen him at Rosie's. Kind of funny to see him both places. Hadn't Critter asked if Dad had seen any strangers?

Why would Critter question Gran about the robberies? What did they have to do with her anyway? My memory flashed to the wad of money in her purse.

Critter stood. "Guess I'll be going now, Rosie. You get in touch if you remember anything, okay?"

Gran stared at the table and finally answered, "Okay."

I'd never heard Gran say anything so short in my life. What had Critter done to her? I shot a look at his back, wishing it could trip him on his way to the door. It didn't work. How dare he get Gran all upset, and on a Saturday night of all times?

Gran excused herself, left the table, and never came back. When Dad went to check on her, he said she had a headache and couldn't join us. The pizza didn't taste quite as good without Gran there to enjoy it with us.

Critter was in big trouble with me.

***

Tuesday afternoon, when I came in from physical therapy, there sat Critter, a huge ham and cheese sandwich on a tray table with a side heap of peanut butter cookies and milk. Gran chatted away about the ladies in her quilting club, while Critter munched on his sandwich, which was nearly too big to fit in his mouth. He had on his deputy's uniform, and clearly had come through the front door again. He might be all deputy-on-duty, but that man sure carried around some fierce hunger, on duty or not. I did not particularly like front-door Critter.

We'd never had so much official police business around here.

I did a slow burn, remembering how Critter had gotten Gran so upset the other night. How could she be so nice to him now?

What in the world was going on? Critter chatting with Gran about her friends? That was like me having coffee with the local mechanic. After I greeted them both, I rolled back to the kitchen for some of the peanut butter cookies I smelled. Again, fresh from the oven in time for me to have warm ones when I got home, something I might need to say a special thanks for. Instead of taking them to my room like usual I lingered, hoping to catch some tidbit in the conversation, which turned out to be harder than I expected. Putting your nose in where it doesn't belong can be difficult.

Gran talked about her quilting ladies in great detail. How Emily had gotten her hair done early before quilting, and that had made her late. How Bessie had cleaned her house spick-and-span and baked the best Italian Cream Cake from the secret recipe her great-aunt left behind, and Bessie never shared with anybody. Critter seemed deep in his lunch but made notes about what Gran said.

Then Gran answered some question about the view out the window onto Old Man Clinton's property and barn, how it was so close to Bessie's driveway. My stomach dropped. He was questioning her! About Old Man Clinton's robbery. We'd just heard about that while we were out.

Didn't Gran know about incriminating herself, that she should be getting a lawyer? Didn't she watch true crime television at all? What if Critter checked her purse? My stomach clenched like a fisherman's fist on a pole when he catches the big one.

The conversation continued a good while, with Critter asking a lot of questions in a soft voice I couldn't hear, as if he suspected I was listening in from the kitchen. Maybe I'd been too quiet and given myself away to the ace detective. Maybe Critter acted like his corn bread wasn't all the way done in the middle, but was actually really sharp, and that was his way of making people get comfortable and drop their guard. Maybe I should charge in there and save Gran.

I tried harder to hear, rolled closer to the doorway separating the two rooms, but not close enough so they could see me.

Max's enthusiasm at being home made it even harder to hear everything Critter said. Max stayed quiet when we were at appointments, and then wanted to chatter and get lavished with attention when he got home. I didn't know how to shush Max without giving myself away.

"We think it happened around the time you ladies were together over at Bessie Lee's working on those quilts." Critter had still kept his voice really low, but that came through clearly because Max had finally settled down, just in time it seemed. I was about to rush in and tell Gran to demand a lawyer, but by the time I peeked around the corner it was too late.

Gran had moved over on the sofa beside him, and talked in the softest voice, like she knew I was listening from the kitchen. How long could they talk about a few burglaries anyway?

Finally, the front door closed, and Gran appeared in the kitchen. At least she hadn't left in handcuffs. Had Critter connected her to the burglary at Old Man Clinton's barn? What kind of trouble had Gran gotten herself into by answering his questions? Didn't she understand that she was a suspect?

CHAPTER TWELVE

Time dragged. It had been hard to concentrate on much since I'd seen Gran so upset at the restaurant with Critter and *nobody* would talk about why, least of all Gran, who loved to talk about nearly anything. Usually, I couldn't get her to shut up. And then he'd questioned her at the house too. I had to find out about these robberies. But, how?

I closed my spirit journal, my eyes crossed from so much research this week, trying to get my mind off my worries. Harlan would love this place I was researching—and it was close enough that we might talk Uncle Ezra into getting us there soon. Another old haunted hospital, Sun Valley, had been one of Momma's favorites in the area. It wasn't as famous as our property, but infants died there, and Momma said their sweet baby souls lingered.

I'd researched topics for our episodes for the remainder of the year—we only had about fifteen episodes left until we started a new year. Sometimes we changed plans when something exciting happened, like a sighting somewhere, but Harlan and I both liked to have an idea about what we'd film.

Once our followers had passed 5,000, we got serious. People depended on us to post new information, and hearing from followers kept us motivated to do more and better. We hoped someday to travel and film the actual hot spots we'd only seen in pictures. We had a list of our top ten sites ready to go. Momma had gotten us a good start before she . . . I couldn't stand to use that word. "Before she left us" sounded like she abandoned us out of the blue. Someone should invent a nice word for "passing away" so the words could come out of my mouth without choking me.

My video-cam, safely hidden under the bed, was a constant reminder that something exciting was about to happen. I was dying to get it set up in our cemetery, sure the new technology was good enough to catch some spirits on it. Praying it would be Momma we caught. Relieved that Harlan shared the secret.

I'd been overcome with curiosity and taken a glance at the directions. Waiting for Harlan to set it up with me seemed like a good idea, a great idea in fact. Two would handle it better than one—there were a lot of settings involved. I texted Harlan.

Can't wait to set up the camera!

Seriously!

I hoped he was being sincere. *Mean it?*

On board.

Did you see comment from GhostRyder on our blog post? New Orleans Cem. post.

Not yet.

See if you want to add anything to my answer.

Looks good to me. You covered it.

OK. What r u working on?

Sorry. Gotta go.

What now? This happened all the time with Harlan. I'm not sure his dad even knew he had his own phone—Harlan had told me his dad didn't believe in cell phones, said they were an extravagance that normal people didn't need. His phone plan was on his uncle's account, and he hadn't had it very long. After his dad had screamed in the background a few times when we talked, Harlan quit talking on the phone, and only texted. No video chats ever. He'd been here a million times. Despite being best friends, I'd never been to his house. We'd never talked about it, but I'd heard rumors about his dad being a "recluse" and mad all the time. Seems like having a kid like Harlan would give him nothing to complain about.

Wednesday at dinner Gran looked cheerful again, smiling and chirpy, like the morning robins. She'd been quiet ever since Critter got her so upset. I gulped and brought up the topic—but sort of sideways.

"Glad your headache's finally better, Gran," I started. She snapped her head in my direction, but only after a quick glance at Dad.

"I'm fine. You don't need to worry about me." She left the table, clearing her plate even though she'd barely touched it.

"What was it Critter was talking to you about?"

Gran slowly turned and her eyes looked red, like she might've dripped a few tears. "We were just chatting about all those robberies that have been going on." She turned her back on me to slam some dishes around in the sink.

Dad shook his head in a firm *no* and that was the end of that. Uncle Ezra walked over and put an arm around Gran. Guess I'd have to get my answers somewhere else, maybe from that snake, Critter.

Like magic, a knock sounded from the front door, and when Dad opened it, Critter's voice carried to the kitchen. "I'm here for Gran."

"I told you—" Dad started before Critter cut him off.

"I'm doing you a favor. If I take her now, Judge Warren is going to meet us and set bail. She won't have to stay overnight at the jail."

The jail! The jail! Gran seemed to stagger at the sink. Uncle Ezra led her over to the table. I knew we couldn't trust Critter!

"How could they possibly think I . . . Scooter, you know I wouldn't . . ." Gran put her head down on the table and cried.

I patted her hand. "Don't you worry, Gran. We'll get Critter arrested. He can't do this to you."

Dad appeared in the doorway, his eyes shiny and shook his head. "You heard him," he said as soon as he saw us. He walked over and hugged Gran. "Let's get this over with so we can get you back home where you belong."

Behind Dad, Critter appeared. If only my eyes could dart deadly rays at him. Gran wiped her eyes, pulled herself up from the chair, and held out her wrists to Critter.

"I'm not going to put these cuffs on you, Gran. I don't have a choice about taking you in, but I do have control of that."

Gran smiled at Critter. She followed him and Dad out of the house.

The days really dragged after that. Gran came back home but refused to discuss it. Life in our house had never been so silent.

Thursday—check. Friday—check. My calendar hadn't added any dates this week but it sure felt like it. The week dragged forever. I tried with Dad, Uncle Ezra, and Gran—no one would talk about Gran's arrest or the robberies.

"If you ask one more question, Scooter Marie, I'll ground your electronics for a month," Dad shouted one night at dinner.

Gran left the table in tears. I shut up and shut

down. Guess I'd leave the robberies up to them for now.

Everywhere we went in town people turned away and whispered in that way we have around the hollow. People think it's more polite. Some people treated us like the kinfolk who moved to Detroit to get away from here—unwanted. We'd show them when we found the real robber. But, most of our friends hugged us or gave us sad looks.

I had plenty to do while I looked for a way to help Gran—Momma's clock was ticking still, and I needed to help her. At least trying to find her was in the works. We'd be filming spirits soon.

Harlan and I stayed busy with our channel and blog, but we were both dying to get the camera going. I wouldn't see him until "work" on Saturday. Seems like that's why Dad started paying us to begin with, because "working" meant Harlan could at least spend Saturdays with us. Once in a while Dad managed to get him for extra "work" in the summer, but not too often.

Finally, Saturday took a turn on my calendar. Harlan and I couldn't wait for the paintballers to get out on the field so we could look at the camera together. The instruction book made it look complicated, but Harlan was a genius with technology. This was our chance to reach Momma, or at least catch old Zeb in action out there in the cemetery, since I hadn't caught him on film in the house and he hadn't been back. Mounting the camera would be a big job, and we'd only have a few hours before someone would come looking for us tomorrow. So, the more we understood today, the better it would be tomorrow.

We'd gotten permission to film a YouTube video in our cemetery on Sunday. That would give us a chance to set up the spirit camera, but I wasn't ready to tell Dad about that quite yet. We often filmed our segments there because of the old tombstones and the known fact of our cemetery and property's spookiness. We'd actually film a video while we were there, too, so the filming excuse wouldn't be a big fat lie, which I was generally opposed to, even though I lied when I thought it didn't matter once in a while. Harlan, however, would never be part of a direct lie to Dad.

With the box at our feet, Harlan skimmed the directions, studied the camera settings, twisted dials, and finally smiled, apparently satisfied. Genius!

"We're good to go." Harlan loaded everything back in the box. "Aren't you going to thank me?"

"Thank you, oh master of the ghost hunting universe, technician extraordinaire, all-knowing guide to the spirits, for your services today." I loaded as much sarcasm as I could into my voice. Sometimes he got a little too big for his britches and needed to be teased out of it so he didn't get all uppity about being so smart. I was plenty smart, but not as patient with stuff like steps and directions. If it didn't happen fast, I wasn't the girl for the job.

Reckon I could've done it, but in twice the time, maybe three times, if I'm to be honest. And I'd probably throw the box across the room in frustration by the time I'd finished. I *think* I could've anyway, but that's why Harlan and I made a great team. My genius at words—talking, researching, and presenting our research on YouTube—were a perfect match for his genius with photography. My tech skills weren't shabby, but his skills with photography and technology were awesome. I couldn't get too interested in the details of photography. I left that up to Harlan. But I could crush him at chess, which required a different kind of strategic thinking.

"I'll bring some tools and stuff we might need to mount it. I think it'll fit in my backpack tonight when I leave." Harlan motioned to his ever-present blue backpack, resting nearby with Max curled around it.

"What do I need to do?" I asked. I needed to do my full share of the work, since he'd have the harder job tomorrow.

"You be ready to do the YouTube filming totally on your own. That way I can concentrate on *this* camera. Destination: Coordination!" He slapped a high five at our team cheer, once again back to our full team spirit.

The shouts and clatter of men approaching the store startled us.

"Hey, another robbery over at Lanesville," a voice shouted. "Just got a text."

I'd almost forgotten about the robberies, about my worries about Gran, about the outside world. Somehow, when I was here, I left my troubles behind. It was the one place I could forget my sunburned soul and act normal. Reality hit me like a falling oak. Another robbery! Hopefully Gran's work at the restaurant would give her an alibi.

The clomp of boots inside the door alerted us

that we'd been so involved in our studies of the camera that we'd missed the first few people coming inside. A few lined up at the window, already waiting on us. How did we miss the slam of that door? The time had flown! We shoved the box into Harlan's backpack and moved it aside.

"Grab a pop for Walter and I'll get the window." I wheeled over to the equipment window and got busy. As usual, everyone hit the field at about the same time when we opened and returned in a huge rush, getting their money's worth until the last minute. All except Walter, who usually not only got started late, but came in from the fields early, and hung around a while. Come to think of it, Walter hadn't come in early today unless he had put his stuff on the counter and left quietly, which didn't seem likely. That was more Creepy Pete's style.

Finally, we finished. I caught Harlan's gaze, and we rolled our eyes at each other after the last car pulled out of the lot. We hustled to get the equipment cleaned and repaired and back in the bins—ready for this busy day to end. At least it hadn't been as crazy as last week with the competition.

"Where's my pop?" The voice boomed in the nearly empty store.

Harlan and I jumped to look behind us. Walter. We'd thought everyone was gone. Max hadn't warned us that anybody was in the store, but he knew Walter, who always brought him a treat. Walter's return to the station this late in the day was unusual. Where had he been?

"I'll get it now," Harlan said. "We put it back in the cooler when you didn't show up at your usual time."

Walter's hair stuck out all over and his face flushed red, glistening with sweat. He shook his head and smoothed his hair back. "I . . . ran into an old friend and caught up on old times." He handed over his paint gun and visor and waited for his pop. "There he is now."

The new guy's camouflage had a stiff crease in the legs of the pants—too new and neat for our grubby battlefield. He looked more like a banker than a gamer. Walter motioned him closer for an introduction. It was the same person who I called Panda, the new guy I'd noticed watching Dad last week.

"Have you met my favorite rascals around here yet? Scooter's daddy is the one I told you about who runs the place, and old Harlan here is another right-hand man." We both shook hands with the too-neat-looking man. No sweat, no dirt, not a speck of paint on him. Chills shook my body from head to toe, something I couldn't explain. Max might not have alerted us to Walter, but his low throaty growl told me he'd noticed this stranger. If Max didn't like him, then neither did I.

"Sorry, I didn't get your name, sir." I smiled my most innocent smile. I didn't trust strangers, not since a drunk stranger plowed into our car and took Momma. My gut churned and I shivered more in the increasing chill, like a negative spirit had invaded our space. Max continued his low throaty growl, a vibration more than a sound, but he paced now too.

"Nick Ashford, from over by Florenceville. This is some place you got here."

"So, did you like the games?" I asked. Harlan had returned with Walter's pop, and I felt better with him beside me. He patted Max and raised his eyebrows at me.

Harlan followed my gaze at the new guy's clean pants. His wrinkled forehead showed he wondered the same thing I did: how had he been out on the fields with Walter, who dripped sweat and sported paint splatters, while Panda could pose for a magazine? And his shoes. Not a speck of mud!

"I'm just learning the ropes. I mostly watched today. Next time I'll get a little paint going. I owe Walter here a few good hits." He slapped Walter's back in emphasis. Walter didn't smile, like a friend might have. The chill must have hit him too.

The door slammed and Harlan's Uncle Sonny bustled in. Uncle Sonny looked like a flamingo in a pigpen. His neatly trimmed hair and dark suit with blue tie would be perfect for church. He had probably been showing houses to some rich clients. Since the car factory had settled near a neighboring town, his real estate business had been booming. People didn't seem to mind driving twenty miles to and from work if they got the property they wanted. The new jobs had mountain folks staying instead of leaving for better opportunities like they normally did.

I tried to signal to Uncle Sonny the feeling I had—like we needed to watch out for a mountain lion. The chills had morphed into a spider crawl up the spine. I didn't want to say anything out loud. Uncle Sonny kept his gaze steady on mine for a long minute.

The grown-ups exchanged greetings all around.

"I just dropped by to see if you needed a ride," Uncle Sonny said, and draped an arm around Harlan's shoulder. He'd caught my look. I knew because he raised an eyebrow at me and shrugged his shoulders. He didn't know what game he was in, but he'd do his best to play.

"Can we drop him off later? He's earned some pizza!" Dad said from across the room.

"Sure. I'll catch you later, Harlan! Call me if you need anything, you hear me?" Uncle Sonny caught and held Harlan's gaze. Harlan's eyes glistened, and he nodded. I wish Harlan would talk to me about whatever it was they were signaling each other.

Wonder what that was all about? Harlan turned away from me. His Uncle Sonny walked out the door with one last glance over his shoulder at me, not Harlan, like he wasn't sure what his next move should be. My gut twisted over these men whose behavior seemed so off, and that secret between Harlan and his uncle. And Gran. Always Gran.

Walter and his friend followed him out without another word. Nick handed Walter a menu from Rosie's before they were out the door. That seemed really weird.

Dad and Uncle Ezra's presence on the other side of the office was the only thing keeping my heart from racing. The air felt thick today, like an evil spirit darkened it. I didn't like people appearing out of nowhere the way Walter had. Creepy Pete was bad enough at that. Harlan avoided looking at me after his uncle left, and something in his eyes told me to leave it alone. It bugged me that I didn't know what, but I could guess. Something must have happened with his dad. Bet his dad had locked him out again— that happened every so often. And Gran, poor Gran. It was all too much.

But, mostly the strangeness of Walter and Panda slammed me in the face like a runaway paintball. What was Walter's big hurry to leave today? He'd acted so fidgety when he came in from the fields. He usually exchanged a few words with Dad and Uncle Ezra. And his friend's shoes hadn't had a speck of paint or mud on them. And why was he sharing Gran's menu?

My thoughts scrambled like overcooked eggs.

CHAPTER THIRTEEN

We piled into the van, excited to surprise Gran, hoping for a better night than the last time we surprised her at the restaurant. She'd surprised us that time—by leaving. When we got near town, traffic was backed up, which never happened. There was seldom much traffic to speak of. We only had stop signs, not even one red light in our tiny center of town. People poured into town on Saturday nights to the restaurants. Dad said hard-working mountain people needed to have a break on the weekends besides church. Friday and Saturday night for fun—Sunday to be sorry and pray. But even

Saturday night crowds didn't stop traffic.

"Look at that. What's going on?" Harlan craned his neck out the open window. The short block of storefronts in the center of downtown held Gran's place—Rosie's, Sid's Barbershop, The Book Nook, and The Suds Shoppe, which was *not* a laundromat. The tattooed owner of The Suds Shoppe didn't match the image the name made you picture either. Something like Spike's Saloon would fit him better.

But Gran's neon sign wasn't the only thing flashing colors as we turned the corner. A trooper's car, a sheriff's car, and a few volunteer firefighters' cars all flashed their lights outside of Rosie's. Max whimpered and I wanted to whimper, too. A heavy feeling overcame me, and I stifled a groan.

"You don't get that kind of gathering around here unless, . . ." Uncle Ezra said. That much official light power in our small town meant disaster. I prayed Gran was okay. Everybody in town considered her their grandmother, but she was mine. I couldn't stand it if anything happened to her. Getting arrested had been bad enough—even though I was almost sure she'd never rob anybody.

Dad slammed to a halt a block from Gran's—too many official vehicles blocked the way. He and Uncle Ezra took off running. "Catch up with us, Harlan," Dad called back.

Harlan slid the van into a space like a pro, then lowered the lift, and unloaded me. Like most kids in these parts, Harlan had been driving on private property since he was about twelve. My legs itched to catch up to Dad and Uncle Ezra. I clenched my jaw, kept my frustration to myself. In front of Rosie's one of the deputies talked to a few people. Where was Gran?

The rest of us eavesdropped on the conversations around us while I kept an eye on Dad. Soon a deputy lifted the rope and let Dad through to talk to Critter. Uncle Ezra hovered near Dad, but bounced and paced. They must have thought they were protecting me by leaving me with Harlan, but I hated being treated like a baby—or like I couldn't do things everybody else did!

On our side of the street, Harlan left me at the curb where I could watch the entrance to the restaurant. He skirted in and out of the crowd talking to people. While he moved around so freely, I couldn't. People had pushed in front of me. Bodies surrounded my wheelchair, pinning me in. On every side bodies rammed close, jostling each other and me—solid as a brick wall. At butt-height I inhaled odors from the thickened air. I threw my head back, searching for space, for fresh air. Up, up, past the shoulders and heads of strangers, early stars gifted that special magic of twilight. That calmed my pounding, panicked heart for now, but I needed Dad.

A year ago, I could've run over and been with Dad, or at least not been boxed in like this. I'd never minded being in crowds before, but nowadays I wanted to be able to move my wheelchair when I needed to, and getting a wheelchair through a crowd was a lot harder than weaving a body through one. Impossible, actually. I recognized the heartbeat of panic.

A shadow hovered over my chair. I closed my eyes and swallowed my tears before I craned my neck to look at Harlan, who had returned. He knelt down next to me. Put a strong hand on mine.

"Gran got robbed," Harlan said. Quickly, almost in one breath, "She's going to be okay."

I stared at him. I heard the words but couldn't get them to make sense in my brain.

Harlan cleared a path to get me in front again. Across the street the deputies pushed back some of the gawkers. Dad still rocked on his heels. Even with his back to me, his shoulders showed tension, and he ran his fingers through his hair over and over.

Harlan knelt beside me again. "She's already been ambulanced to the hospital. She was knocked out when they found her. No one knows exactly what happened."

"Why are Dad and Uncle Ezra staying over there then? They should go to Gran."

Harlan stood back up and bounced on his toes, trying to get a better look across the street.

"Reckon that robber is in this crowd?" I asked. "Cause I'd sure like to get my hands on him. And, on Critter. Hope he's feeling good and guilty about arresting Gran."

Uncle Ezra rushed up to us, "The store sign had never flipped to OPEN, so someone went around back to check on Gran, and found the door open, her cashbox gone, and Gran out cold on the floor. She'd probably been there since she got there this afternoon."

Poor Gran lying there out cold! I hoped someone would be whisked off to jail in handcuffs tomorrow—or worse.

"Reckon that robber better stay away if he knows what's good for him," I muttered. Tears poured. I didn't care anymore. I couldn't lose Gran. Not now, especially not now.

I spotted Dad returning, shaking his head, still running his hands through his already messy hair. It took a lot to rattle Dad. A Marine, he'd seen action "before I was a twinkle in his eye"—he always stood tall and stiff like the drill sergeants trained him, but now he slumped. Children, dogs, and old ladies—they needed protection. He didn't tolerate anybody creating problems for the helpless. And, Gran, if someone hurt Gran, I don't know what he'd do.

He knelt down in front of me and put both of his hands on mine. "I guess you know she was robbed. Gran's in the hospital. Just a precaution because she likely hit the floor when she fell, or maybe got hit on the head." Dad stood and kicked some loose concrete off the sidewalk. "Who in this holler don't love Gran?"

"Cryin' shame, you ask my opinion." We all turned at the same time to see that the pronouncement had come from Creepy Pete, standing behind our little group on the sidewalk.

Where had he come from? He stood there for a second, and then zigzagged his way toward the corner and disappeared out of sight. Okay. What was up with that?

Nobody wanted to eat now. Dad hitched a ride to the hospital with a deputy and left Uncle Ezra to get Harlan and me home.

Uncle Ezra drummed his fingers on the steering wheel and muttered under his breath. Harlan stared out the window, but he kept my hand in his.

Uncle Ezra made a U-turn before he got to Harlan's house. "We need to feed you, Harlan. Almost forgot. I know you're upset right now, but you might feel like eating a little something later."

Harlan didn't deny his hunger either, like his normal good manners might've made him, so I knew his stomach whooshed with emptiness, else he'd have said never mind. Or maybe his cupboards were bare.

Max put his head on my knees. I buried my face in his fur. Inhaled his dog-smell and dove in for another whiff. My heart raced a little slower. I reached for my necklace—it was gone! My butterfly necklace! If it had been any other time, I'd have made Uncle Ezra turn around and go back and look. But I knew he needed to get me home so he could get to the hospital to check on Gran.

I didn't want to have to search for Gran as a spirit too. I couldn't stand to lose someone else I loved so soon. What kind of person would hurt Gran?

CHAPTER FOURTEEN

The floors creaked. The wind whistled through the cracks of the doors. The hairs on my arms stood up. Any minute I expected another light show from Zeb. Spirits didn't spook me, but today something had my alarms clanging, and I wanted to figure out what. Sometimes being a "sensitive" was scary. I figured either Zeb was trying to break through again, Momma needed me, or Gran was in trouble.

Max paddled his feet in his sleep, probably chasing a dream squirrel through the woods. I hadn't been left alone in the house since . . . well, ever, now that I thought about it. Dad and

Uncle Ezra had been taking turns at the hospital with Gran until the phone rang this morning and Uncle Ezra left in a hurry, leaving me alone with a warning to stay out of trouble.

I reached for my necklace and remembered again that it was gone. Maybe I hadn't lost it last night after all. Maybe I'd lost it here at the house or at work. I searched my bed in case it had broken in my sleep. No necklace. While I was at it, I straightened the covers a little, hard to do from the chair, but I didn't have enough balance to stand and reach. I'd taken it for granted that Dad or Gran always kept my bed fresh and comfy for me.

I searched all through the house for my necklace, scanning the floors for the glitter of gold. Max trailed behind, snuffing along like he knew we needed to find something. No necklace, but Gran had allowed a few dust bunnies to escape. She'd be humiliated.

I followed the path to the paintball store, scanning for it, but the wind blew as if it would pick me up like a kite and swoosh me away to heaven. The grass on the sides of the path flattened with the force. I got lost in the sensation of something besides pain and heartbreak.

Halfway back to the house the clouds opened, and I couldn't see my hand in front of my face with the downpour of rain and darkness. *Run*, my brain screamed. Yeah, right. I laughed until my eyes leaked.

The controls were drowned in water before I remembered to protect them. The chair stalled. Max ran all around me in circles, barking like he was calling for help. A part of me wanted to laugh at him but the other part of me wiped the rainy tears off my face. I took a deep breath, shoved the control with one hand, while I tried to shield it from the rain with the other. The rain was so dense that I bumped the ramp before I realized I'd arrived. Bumped it hard. Thank goodness I didn't turn over.

Once inside, I rushed to change into dry clothes. Dad would kill me if he found out I'd been out wandering around alone with nobody at home. I dried down the Zoomster and last of all Max, who'd been drenched. At least his wet coat I could explain since everyone knew Max loved to play in the rain.

The afternoon alone gave me too much time to think. I sat on the front porch and practiced chords on the guitar. The rain made its own kind of plop-tap-plop music, which sounded a lot better from the porch than being stuck in it. Momma loved storms, and we'd spent many stormy afternoons in the porch swing because she wanted me to love storms too. We never asked the rain to go away.

Maybe my brain got a little waterlogged because, somehow, I thought it might be a good idea to call Critter. I waited for him to come to the phone. What would I even ask?

"Scooter! Are you okay?" Critter's voice sounded three notes higher than usual.

"I'm fine. Sorry if I worried you."

"Thank goodness. They said you had an emergency, and I just saw the boys at the hospital with Gran. What's wrong?"

"I didn't say I had an emergency! They made that part up. Have you caught the person who hurt Gran?" Tears threatened to pour again. I took a deep breath. "I want him in jail now."

"Scooter, it doesn't work like that. It might take some time." Critter's voice now sounded like he was singing a lullaby, but I wasn't some baby.

"Aren't you having a come-to-Jesus moment

along about now? Don't you feel rotten for what you did?"

"Oh, Scooter, I never meant no harm to Gran. I did everything I could to help her."

"I won't never forgive you for what you did. I thought you were good people. But you're worse than a . . . worse than a tick on a hound dog."

I ended the call. Before I said the things I really wanted to say about him arresting Gran. He was clearly going to be no help at all.

At five o'clock Dad's voice echoed from the kitchen. I thought he was talking to someone on the phone as he came into the house, until I heard Uncle Ezra answer him. I raced to the kitchen.

"Has something happened to Gran?" Why hadn't one of them stayed with her? What if that person found her there?

"Gran is fine. She'll be home soon. She insisted we come have dinner with you." Uncle Ezra unloaded paper bags from our favorite burger place.

"I need to find out who hurt her."

Dad glared at me. "What you need to do is

take care of yourself and not give Gran any need to worry."

"But, Critter—"

"Critter called me. You need to let Critter do his job and leave him alone. He didn't hurt Gran. He's trying to help. He doesn't need to be interrupted by your questions." Dad slammed the plates in his hand onto the table with a clatter. "You need to stay out of the way."

The thought of eating made my stomach churn. Dad had never talked to me like that. I turned my chair and went back to my room. I couldn't do anything right these days.

I missed Momma.

CHAPTER FIFTEEN

I thought you'd never get here," I called before Harlan reached the bottom of the steps. I'd been waiting on the front porch, strumming a few chords on the guitar. Gran was heavy in my heart today. I'd probably get to see her tonight. I hoped so—even if it was only for a quick hug. Dad said she was going to be fine, but they were keeping an eye on her at the hospital for now. Would he keep bad news from me? Surely, they'd let her come home soon. Doubts crept in, memories of other hospital stays, and bad endings.

Harlan snapped me back with his answer. "I had to sneak out. Hope I don't get caught." Harlan smoothed the top of his hair, which still glistened with a few drops clustered on top of his tight curls.

"Won't your dad be mad?"

Harlan shrugged. "He's at work now, but I couldn't leave until he left. I'll be home before he gets back. Should be okay."

Harlan and I'd been looking forward to setting up the camera since the package arrived, but we had to wait for the right time. All this robbery stuff couldn't distract me from helping Momma. We needed to find her to help her, or at least find a spirit connection to her.

Harlan worried Dad might be mad if he knew about me spending all that money without permission. Since I wasn't sure how Dad might react, it was best to find the right time and way to tell him—especially now. He didn't know many details about our work for the channel. He'd never objected to any of that work or expense, and this was part of that work, but he seemed pretty stressed lately.

I couldn't hold a straight face and lie, and besides, flat-out lying was wrong. I wasn't opposed to stretching the truth like a rubber band, or not sharing every boring detail. People are so not interested in boring details, especially grown-ups when kids are telling them. They tune us out about half the time anyway. I'd figure a way to handle it as soon as Gran got home.

"We don't need to go in," I said, and sat the guitar down.

Harlan raised an eyebrow and stared. "You didn't tell him, did you?" Harlan gave me one of those looks he specialized in that could usually make me feel guilty.

I took off, hoping he'd follow.

The door creaked open behind us. "You kids be back before dinner," Dad called from the doorway.

"Yessir," Harlan shouted back, then raced ahead with Max, like he'd never been outside on a sunny day before. The sun glinting off his watch cast a flash of bright light.

Harlan and I had permission to spend a few hours out at the cemetery filming for a special YouTube edition of haunted cemeteries. We planned to include our graveyard in a series about haunted burial sites all over the world, from Forest Lawn Memorial Gardens in Florida to the Paris Catacombs in France. So, our double duty for today would make it easier. Harlan would set up the camera while I filmed part of our special. Destination: Coordination—teamwork all the way.

We'd decided our best bet was to mount the camera on the side of the bus facing the cemetery and Momma's grave. The camera had been adapted by professional ghostbusters to detect visible, infrared, and ultraviolet wavelengths. I'd splurged for the special mount, thinking all along that the side of the bus would work. I was relieved when Harlan agreed. I'd gotten a state-of-the-art battery-operated camera, although there was still always the danger of interference from the energy of the spirits, which no one understood. We had extra batteries in case the spirits drained them. If batteries didn't work, we could adapt it and run heavy duty outdoor electrical cords, but we opted to try this first. Electrical cords would be hard to hide.

Momma's headstone and grass and flowers looked too neat and still. If only I'd see something that showed her spirit. "Momma, I know you're here, and I'm sorry we can't talk yet. I'll be ready when you can. Please show me a sign." Max stayed quiet at my side, rubbing his head on my knee. Harlan stayed quiet too, but his lips moved. Maybe a prayer, or a quiet talk with Momma. We stayed quiet and waited. But nothing moved, nothing changed.

The Appalachian Mountains surrounded us like a hug today. Clear blue skies against the green of the trees. Soon they'd be orange, yellow, and red. Tourists would flood the hills. Momma's one-year anniversary was not far off. I stared hard at her headstone, talked to her. "Momma, Gran got robbed. I'm scared. Dad is mad at me. I need you so much."

Harlan watched me closely. I held his gaze without crying. He patted my hand, and then smoothed the grass over Momma, like touching us both would bring us together somehow.

We sat, quiet and sad together, in our little spot in this beautiful hollow. Tears leaked out for a while.

Finally, Harlan broke the silence. "You talk to Zeb and explain to him what we're doing while I do the mounting." I hadn't considered that Zeb might not appreciate what we were about to do. Glad Harlan thought of that.

Sometimes talking to a ghost helps bring them out. Maybe it would at least make Zeb comfortable with us near his resting place. It had been exciting to see him in what seemed to be a fit of temper, but it wouldn't be our first choice for how to meet him up close and personal. If he could control electricity like he had that night, his powers must be fearsome.

I glanced at my watch. Already an hour gone, and we hadn't even gotten started. If we were gone more than a few hours, someone would come looking for us. We didn't want anybody nosing around here while we worked. So, we jumped right in and got busy.

I set up the iPad that we used to film our videos with the app that allowed us to load them straight to YouTube, and glanced through my notes. Harlan hated being on camera because he minded if he made a mistake and got flustered. I didn't have any shyness with filming. I loved the camera and didn't worry about mistakes. No one could see me from the waist down, most times, and my chair only showed when we did action filming. Otherwise, it was just head and shoulders. I felt like my old self on camera. And I guess I had a tad bit of Uncle Ezra's vanity. I wish I had his gorgeous hair. Instead I got Dad's cowlicks in my mousy brown hair. Oh, well, even that didn't hold me back from my love for the camera.

Go time. For YouTube we'd talk about Zebediah, even though we most hoped to catch Momma's spirit. That would be too personal to share. That spirit was private, just for me and Harlan.

Hi, everybody, it's Scooter and Harlan filming today in our old family cemetery. I've been told all my life that it's haunted, and I believe I know at least one of the spirits who visits this area, my great-, great-, great-grandfather who served in the Civil War, and is buried right here. He built some of the original buildings on this property and died much too young. It was said that he frequently came back in spirit to visit the eight children he left behind. I believe it's true. I'd like to find video proof of Zeb, and we'll be sure to let you know if we do. Hang with me while I try to communicate with Zebediah to let him know what we're doing. We don't want to upset him or disrespect his resting place.

I took the tintype photograph from my pocket. I'd snuck it from the family Bible case. Dad would kill me if he found out. It was one of our family's treasures. But it *might* act as a trigger to bring Zeb out. It takes a lot of energy for a spirit to manifest, and he'd been gone a long time. Maybe this beautiful photograph of his young wife would help him come visit us in a better frame of mind, or spirit.

Sitting very still, I told Zeb my story, with the camera still running.

Zeb, you've been to see me at the house. I think you were warning me about something, but I don't know what. Or maybe you were trying to give me a message from Momma, a brand-new spirit in your world. Except that you seemed angry, and Momma wouldn't have made you angry because she's a sweet soul. We hope we can see you on this camera we're setting up and understand your message if you have one. I'll leave Priscilla's picture here for you for a while. It will be right on the bus, waiting for you whenever you want to come. If you see Momma, give her a butterfly kiss from me, and tell her I miss her so much. Whenever she can come see me, I'm ready. I won't be scared, promise. Bye now, Zeb. And I hope you come see us soon.

A short pause followed, out of respect for Zeb, and then I spoke to the audience to close the video.

That's it, everybody. Thanks for being with us today. Tune in next week when we'll continue discussing haunted cemeteries. If you want to do some fun research, check out the St. Louis Cemetery No. 1 in New Orleans, Louisiana. Be sure to like, subscribe, comment, and share. You know we love to hear from you, so tell us your favorite cemetery stories. Bye, now.

See you next week, same time, same channel for our (I paused, and Harlan popped in) presentation from your favorite ghost hunters.

"What do you think?" I asked Harlan, putting down the mic.

"Great! They'll love it! Glad you let them know we'd be live today." He wound cords around his arm. "Give me a minute to finish up and we'll head back."

I waited with Max in the warm sunshine while Harlan finished up. It didn't take him much longer, but he did a lot of testing to be sure the camera recorded okay. And it didn't. At first.

When his first few tests didn't work, I figured I'd kissed $400 goodbye. That would be fun to explain! He made adjustments that I admitted I didn't understand—he not only loved the technology of photo-printing but studied photography on his own by watching online tutorials. That combination saved the day. He got a test run he was happy with, and said we'd have to wait and see.

We still had time left before we needed to be back, so we threw the tennis ball for Max for a while before we headed to the house. Max could do that for hours, but we forgot to bring him any extra water today like we usually do. Max's panting reminded me again that he could have heat stroke if he got overheated, and I'd never take any chances with him. One time he'd gotten overheated on a walk with Dad and was sick for a week.

I called Max and tilted my water bottle to give him the last little bit. He lapped the stream of water— every last drop I had in my bottle. Clearly, he was still thirsty. I needed to get better at bringing water for him, and a bowl. He didn't get enough from my bottle for the amount of running around he'd done in the hot sun.

Harlan glanced at his watch. "Time to head back."

I threw one last glance at Momma's headstone. Not even a butterfly today. Maybe the heat had made even them find shade.

Harlan's footsteps pounded the blacktop next to me, keeping perfect time to my wheels. A butterfly flitted by. A Cabbage White—Momma's favorite. Maybe she'd felt my sadness after all. I smiled as it joined a mate in the butterfly garden, swirling around each other as the sun threw its warmth and light on us. A warmth spread through me, and not just from the sunshine. Harlan noticed them too and smiled in my direction. Not at the cemetery, but still, this might be from Momma. This was a definite maybe!

The scent of lilac from Momma's butterfly garden drew my attention. The marigolds and butterfly bushes drew butterflies, and I reached to touch my necklace, only it wasn't there. Would I ever find it? With Gran in the hospital I hadn't even mentioned it to anybody except Harlan.

"We did it," Harlan said with a sigh.

"Now we wait."

I said a silent prayer that Zeb would show up. Momma must still be struggling to come back, just getting used to her new spiritual home and all. But at least she sent a signal.

CHAPTER SIXTEEN

"Are you sure you want to do this today?" I asked Gran. She'd amazed all of us with how she'd bounced back so quickly after her robbery. I hadn't even been allowed to visit her before she got released. Not that I wanted to visit a hospital, and maybe that's part of why Dad kept me away.

"I've been looking forward to this for weeks." Gran struggled to keep up with me, so I set a lower speed on the Zoomster.

Cruising the mall had a new meaning: the Zoomster actually cruised. What a celebration to be at the mall with Gran! She'd declared she was fit as a fiddle and ready to do some back-to-school clothes shopping. She had one rule: no talk about the robbery.

Dad and Uncle Ezra stayed busy with the business. They both pleaded ignorance about girl's clothes, and neither of them had ever loved school like I had, or at least I did before the accident.

After I came back from the accident last year, kids acted different. Any time the word "walk" came up in conversation, the kids looked at me like they were afraid I'd melt or throw flames. New kids asked me to play—out of pity, and my old friends avoided me—except Harlan. He said to give them time, that they didn't know what to say because they felt so bad for me.

It would be nice to start at the middle school with some new clothes and with new kids. I cared more about comfort these days, but I still wanted to blend in at the new school—at least as much as I could. Max and the Zoomster would draw enough attention without a clothes disaster. Kids pretty much dressed in jeans and t-shirts, so it should be easy.

Gran snapped the van into the first available space and helped me out. It had been a long drive. Before I knew it, we'd swept through three stores. The racks made walls around me, and I couldn't see a path sometimes. Not a problem—Gran barreled ahead, pulling one thing after another off the rack for my inspection. Whenever we left a store and went into the open air of the mall, I breathed normally. Inside those crowded aisles, not so much.

I only wanted jeans, not skirts, and she said she could live with that after I convinced her by pointing out all the kids in jeans at the mall. With my new stick-legs I'd best keep them covered. Girls wore their skirts too short anyway, Gran said.

She bought me pair after pair of jeans, until she had to run some bags out to the car. I enjoyed people-watching while she was gone and tossed a coin in the fountain to make a wish. It's bad luck to tell your wish, so it was a secret, but I knew it would eventually come true.

Gran handed salespeople her credit card again and again, until I said, "Gran, that's too much!" I'd never realized how expensive clothes were. And she'd just been robbed. I wouldn't even let myself think about the money I'd seen in her purse. It was all too confusing. And now I couldn't take the chance to ask her questions because Dad would kill me if I got Gran upset.

"Not at all. These will last you for a while.

Starting a new school is special and exciting. It's a grand occasion to splurge on new clothes." She grinned from ear to ear.

"Now for some more tops," Gran said. "Or do you want a snack first?"

"A snack!" I'd smelled cinnamon a few stores back.

"A snack it is then."

We headed for some ginormous cinnamon rolls with ooey-gooey icing. We picked the gooiest rolls and asked for extra icing.

"This is even better than I remembered," I mumbled around a mouthful of roll. I hadn't been here since I lost Momma.

We both got quiet for a minute. I guess Gran had her own memories to deal with.

A shadow hung over us. I flinched when Panda hovered at our table. "Hi, there! They let you out of that window sometimes, huh?"

It took me a minute to realize he meant the window where I worked. I introduced him to Gran, and he charmed her for a few minutes before moving on.

After he left, Gran asked, "How exactly do you know him?"

I explained that he was a new paintball customer.

"He seemed very familiar. I can't quite place him."

When we finished our rolls and drinks, Gran patted my hand, and for once I didn't try to snatch my hand away. My chest tightened when I remembered how many times I'd been rude to her. I hadn't wanted her trying to replace Momma in our house. The house had suddenly felt too crowded when she arrived. I had too many changes too fast, and I had wanted things like they used to be. It had taken a while to get used to Gran, and her different ways of doing things.

"I always wanted a girl to shop with. Did you know your Momma and I used to love to shop for your clothes when you were little? She'd come out every season for a one-day splurge with me. We'd shop until we dropped. She loved this place too. We shared lots of cinnamon rolls over the years." A smile split her face again, but a tear dripped out of the corner of her eye.

I realized Gran missed Momma too. I'd been selfish not to think about how much everybody else missed her. Like a turtle, I'd huddled into my own grief and separated myself with a hard shell of leave-me-alone.

I reached to touch my necklace. It was gone. I'd forgotten.

Now that Gran mentioned shopping with Momma, memories of oodles of new clothes appearing after Momma going to town with Gran came flooding back. It's funny how you take things for granted until they disappear. How did I not remember that they shopped for my clothes together?

I arrived back home with so many bags that everybody had to pitch in to get them into my closets and drawers. My heart filled with something warm, something I hadn't felt for a while. Dad, Uncle Ezra, Gran. They all worked so hard to keep our family going. I wanted to keep this feeling going for a while. Safe, secure, together. I could still appreciate them while I missed Momma. Maybe appreciating what I had and enjoying it might help Momma transition to her new spirit world. I don't think she'd want all my sorrows staining the air in our home.

Unfortunately, after they all left, and I remembered the reason for the shopping, I lost that great feeling. I wrote it down to get it out of my head—sometimes that helps.

I have great new clothes, perfect Yoda folders, and my favorite erasable pens—required. I guess all sixth graders make a lot of mistakes, not just me.

But I'm putting up a front about the real way I feel. I'm so worried about making new friends. Maybe I relied on Harlan so much that I didn't care about other friends when all the other kids got busy making them in fourth and fifth grade. Maybe the accident sent me into such a tailspin I didn't care about friendships anymore after that. Maybe I counted on Momma to be my best friend forever. It was lucky Harlan could see inside of me. Even when I was busy fooling everyone else, he always saw the truth and the pain. And stood beside me through it all, never letting me push him away. I don't know what I'd do without him.

Since friend-making might take a while, I better start school with a realistic attitude. I'll survive—that seems enough for a while. Thank goodness I have a few weeks of freedom left.

I sure hope our spirit camera picks something up soon. I'd love it to be Momma! That's my dream, my wish at the fountain, to see Momma. But at least we know Zeb could if he wanted to. We have to be patient like good Jedi and wait for Zeb to show himself when he feels ready. He probably appreciated us giving him some space.

CHAPTER SEVENTEEN

Gran could refuse to talk to me about the robbery, but she couldn't stop me from trying to find the monster who caused her to slam her head so hard to the floor that it knocked her out. Max snuggled at my feet and woofed his agreement. I finally had a day when I could dig in and do some serious research.

I texted Harlan. *Need more details of robberies. Call ur uncle. Get the dirt.* Maybe his uncle would know the latest. He had so many connections around the area.

He didn't answer. That was unusual. He usually did, even if it was TTYL to let me know he was busy. Guess I was on my own.

I booted up my trusty computer, Watson, and got ready to roll with my best investigative skills. Dad and Uncle Ezra were working the VFW fish fry, so I had the night to myself if they could manage to be on their own for a whole night. One of them almost always found an excuse to come home early and make sure all was well, like we couldn't survive one night without them. Just because we'd called them when the fuses blew, and then again when Gran fell that one time, they acted like we couldn't take care of ourselves.

No way did I want Dad to know I was sticking my nose in where it didn't belong, one of his favorite sayings about me. He'd made it clear that he wanted me to leave this alone. He should understand that Gran was my business, and what if they came after us at paintball? I needed to protect us against this guy who went after easy money. He'd love our Saturday stash. We had to be on his radar.

I'd become quite the detective lately, anyway. I'd learned about our wreck by reviewing our local Bugle's online archives. Dad had refused to talk about the accident, insisting that we focus on moving forward, and said I shouldn't dwell on the details of that awful night. Since he teared up every time I tried to ask a question, I quit asking a long time ago. But that didn't mean I quit wondering. Or had left well enough alone, as Gran loved to say.

Watson and I could find our way around an investigation, especially with the web at our fingertips. After all, ghost hunting required investigation too. We researched lots of stuff for YouTube. Haunted houses, haunted cemeteries, haunted hotels, haunted objects. I had been shocked when I'd found so many things relating to spirits when we first started with Momma. I especially loved the scientific studies about things like ESP and telekinesis, other invisible things we can't explain beside spirits. Just because you can't see something doesn't mean it doesn't exist.

And just because the police couldn't find the culprit didn't mean I couldn't try. After all, Yoda had believed that the mind of a child was a wonderful thing, open to possibilities that someone with wisdom might miss. Time for me to give it a shot. I glanced at Yoda and wished for luck.

I clicked my way into the newspaper archives to pin down the dates and details of these robberies. Blake Shelton sang in the background while I compiled a list of robberies within five miles during the last few months:

- *Tim's Pawn Shop, near Shelbyville (Dad's friend but he didn't mention it!??)*

- *Old Man Clinton's Barn, outside of center-town of Chamber's Corner (lots of money there!, Gran nearby—suspect!!!)*

- *Donut Hole on Highway 60 (door unlocked)*

- *Dairy Queen (did Horace make that one up?)*

- *Middleton Pool (kids' prank?)*

- *Gran (time to find this crook!)*

One by one, I listed the names of the stores, the people who'd been robbed . . . I knew them all. My eyes grew wider as I studied my list, my throat closing up as I read and reread each name. My fingers couldn't click fast enough to keep up with my brain that was spinning faster than a tornado. No wonder there was so much talk. When you put this all together, our town had never seen such disrespect in so short a time.

I printed a map of Chamber's Corner with a five-mile radius. I mounted it on my corkboard and pinned each location of a robbery. The pawnshop. Odd that Dad hadn't mentioned it. The news reported that the break-in occurred on a weekend and only items with gold seemed to have been taken, but a lot of them, with huge value. Technically that was a burglary, but I wasn't being technical—they were all robberies to me. Red pin number one.

Then Old Man Clinton's barn while he'd been away visiting his lady friend, Elmira. *Nothing of value taken* meant that Old Man Clinton wasn't about to admit to any reporter snooping around that he kept anything of value in his barn. But the old man bragged to anyone who stopped at his roadside vegetable stand that he'd never be snookered by any new-fangled bank because he buried his money in his own barn where he could keep an eye on it himself. Red pin number two. Likely someone fairly local for this one who knew he visited Elmira on the weekends when he took a short break from his farm chores.

The tap at my door reminded me I wasn't totally alone in the house. Gran bustled in with cookies and milk. Thank the Good Lord she wasn't a carrots and beet juice kind of grandmother!

"Thanks, Gran!" I inhaled the smell of peanut butter. My favorite cookie would soothe my grumpy stomach.

"What's that you're working on, honey?" Gran stared at the map.

"Um, just checking out something for YouTube." I crossed my fingers for the fib. Max looked up at me as if he questioned my answer. Sometimes a vague little fib is faster than an explanation. She'd tell Dad what I was up to if I admitted what I was really doing.

Gran waited for me to talk until she seemed to accept that there would be no chat today. I didn't want to hurt her feelings, but I was on a roll.

As soon as she left, I tried Harlan again, but still no answer. Every once in a while, he'd be out of touch, and then when I saw him again, his usual cheerful self seemed tamped. Like a puppy who's been scolded. He never confided, and I never pushed. I knew he'd return my calls when he could, and that he'd tell me only what he wanted me to know about his life away from us. Sometimes he'd tell me his dad grounded him for no reason, and I knew his dad yelled—a lot. Some things didn't lend themselves to words so well, I reckon. He wouldn't talk to Dad about it either.

I got back to my research while I ate the gooey deliciousness of the warm cookies. I had to admit—Gran was a great cook, and she meant well. She wanted something I couldn't give her—maybe Dad and Uncle Ezra had been more entertaining when they were young. To hear the stories, they probably were. She didn't care so much for ghosts and spirits, and I sure couldn't talk about the robber with her.

Next came the Donut Hole, where cash was taken from the drawer over the weekend. The doors had been left unlocked to make it easy for any wandering thief in need of cash, so no property damage happened there. The sweet little owner, Mr. Gonzales, trusted everybody. Geez, wonder if he left some donuts by the cash drawer so the robber wouldn't get hungry? Pin three.

In the background Blake belted out "Honey Bee" and I tapped my fingertips for a few minutes, remembering how Harlan and I sang a duet to that song last weekend. Country music bonded us too.

I hoped Harlan would get more of the scoop on his end of things, but small-town newspapers tended to print a lot of details you'd never see in big-city newspapers, and neighborhood gossip filled in the rest of the story, so he might not have any more info than what I had.

Horace Snawder had told us about the next one at the Dairy Queen. A back door that didn't lock very well had been jimmied open and the robber got $200 and Horace's birthday ice cream cake. A thief with a sweet tooth.

I'd been sure Horace had made up that whole story when he didn't have a cake at his party. He'd been known to tell a whopper or two in his day. Guess not. Pin four.

The next one could have been a bunch of kids pranking. Someone emptied all of the vending machines of cash at the Middleton indoor community pool—no forced entry and no broken machines.

So many people had keys to that place. And once you got into the building, we all knew where the key ring for the vending machines hung in the office. Again, small-town trust made it too easy.

When you lost money in the machine,

anybody was allowed to retrieve it for you. Those keys saw more action than a squirrel gathering nuts before a winter storm. Surprisingly, the robbers hauled away around $2,500, mostly in quarters. That would have been a big, heavy load. Pin number five.

And then Gran's place got hit. Until Gran, no one had been hurt, and according to her, she hadn't been hurt by the robber, just startled and scared, most likely hurting herself when she fell. Gran got a special blue pin. Number six. That robbery meant the most to me. Scared me to death. Had my temper hot as blue blazes at whoever scared Gran.

If our paintball place were the bull's-eye center of a target, the locations of the robberies formed a wide circle all around, in the ten points section of the dartboard. Hmmm. Someone kept things pretty close to home. I plotted the dates on a calendar. I added the calendar to the corkboard. I sighed and closed my eyes for a second. What a bust! All that time and all I had was a bunch of locations and times of robberies. I didn't see any pattern or have any idea who might've robbed these places. I don't even think I had all the robberies yet. Some happened a little farther away.

"We can do this, boy." I patted Max's wiry back, and slipped him a tiny bite of the cookie, one of his favorites too.

I missed Harlan, and hoped everything was okay, that he wasn't mad at me for something. What if Harlan had outgrown me now that he had gotten so tall and would be in a whole separate hallway at school? I wanted Harlan to help me solve these robberies just like we worked together on our spirits.

I glanced to Yoda for inspiration. "Do or do not. There is no try." Now to figure out what the cops knew about these crimes besides what was in the paper. I *would* solve these robberies— hopefully with Harlan's help. No one could hurt Gran and get away with it.

I went to bed. I'd just drifted off to sleep when I sensed a shadow in my doorway. I'd been having a nightmare about Dad finding out about the camera. In my dream the camera had cost $3,000 and fell on Harlan and killed him. My subconscious was talking to me.

The collision of the dream and Dad in my doorway made the decision easy.

"I need to tell you something," I said, about half asleep.

"It's late. Tell me in the morning."

"No, now. I used all my money to buy a camera to film Momma. I should've told you."

"Well, you've told me now. Have you told your daddy?"

My eyes shot wide open. "Uncle Ezra?"

"Yes. Your daddy had to stay late tonight. I was going to tuck you in, but you looked all settled."

"Please let me tell Dad. He might get upset."

"Good night, Scooter. Go back to sleep. Tomorrow's another day."

CHAPTER EIGHTEEN

Dad agreed to drop me in town to see Gran at work. The ride over seemed like the perfect time to tell him about the camera. I wasn't sure Uncle Ezra would keep it from him, so I'd better get there first.

"Dad, you know how much I believe in spirits?" He was big on having a passion for something.

He glanced over his shoulder at me. "Scooter Marie, we have bigger problems than your silly spirits right now. Knock it off and grow up. There's a robber out there, and people are getting hurt."

Momma had been fond of saying that it was a true miracle she married a Marine, and then she would plant a huge kiss on Dad's cheek. I never saw Momma look at Daddy without a gleam of something in her eyes that I called TRUE LOVE. His eyes didn't look at me with any of that now.

I clamped my lips shut, to stop the tears and my big mouth from pouring unwanted stuff like a hole in a dike. Hadn't he loved Momma, and she loved spirits? They weren't silly to her.

The rest of the ride passed in silence. He'd pretty much given his permission for me to work on the robberies now.

"I'm sorry, baby. I'm a little overwhelmed right now," Dad apologized as he helped me off the van.

I didn't say anything to him and plastered a smile on my face before I went in to see Gran. No need for her to be upset.

"Surprise!" I rolled toward Gran on the far side of the restaurant, where she huddled over a pile of cloth napkins and cutlery.

Her wrinkled frown eased, and she jumped up from her table to greet me.

She and I folded napkins around cutlery

while we talked. Nothing but cloth napkins would do for Gran—she expected folks to show some manners, even when scarfing down her delicious pizzas. Of course, the cutlery was mostly for show, since we all knew that eating pizza correctly meant folding a slice just so in your hands and diving in. Sometimes a health nut ordered a salad. How could they do that when the smell from the huge ancient pizza ovens hit you in the face when you walked in?

We sat at Gran's special table while we worked. The heavy tables had just about every couple in the area's initials carved into them. Dad had carved Momma's initials above his, surrounded by a heart. Gran had moved that table to be "hers" after Momma died. People only used that table when invited by Gran.

Gran's first dollar earned here still hung framed beside the cash register on a wall now planted full of signed one-dollar bills. One day a country music star didn't have anything to sign his autograph on, so Gran handed him a dollar bill to sign, then hung it on the wall. After that, the tradition snowballed, and the wall was covered with signed dollar bills, including my own from when I was in Kindergarten.

At a table in the corner, a college-aged couple

made goofy goo-goo eyes with each other. Their pizza sat in the middle of the table untouched, except the guy eyed the pizza once in a while. But she held his hands in a death grip. Good luck College Joe. Maybe cold pizza for lunch tomorrow. Otherwise the place was mostly empty this time of day. In another couple of hours it would be hard to find a table, and the carryout line would be backing up. You had to wait for a pizza here, but small-town folks don't rush around like city people do, so nobody minded. Waiting lines allowed people to catch up on gossip. Standing around could be a party in itself, especially at Gran's, where she kept weekend lines happy with garlic breadsticks.

"It's been a while since you popped in on your own." Gran wiped her hands on her apron and smoothed my hair. "You're a sight for sore eyes." I was proud of myself when I didn't pull away.

"I wanted to talk to you without Dad around." I gulped, thinking carefully about my next words. I didn't want to make her as upset as I'd made Dad.

"It always is a little crazy at dinner with those two boys of mine around." Gran pushed hair out of her face. "I love having you to myself once in a while."

"Gran, please tell me more about when you were robbed."

She shook her head before I finished the question. "You shouldn't worry your head about things like that, Scooter. Let the grown-ups deal with those problems."

"I can't stand the idea that somebody hurt you." Again, those memories flooded, and tears came close to the surface, but didn't leak out, only because I bit my tongue a little to distract me, a trick I'd learned. I'd had to use that trick a lot this past year. Sometimes until my tongue bled.

Gran stopped what she was doing with the napkins and took both my hands in hers. Her work-rough hands still gripped strong, not weakened by whatever had happened to her. Her strength reassured me that she'd made a good recovery.

"I don't think they *meant* to hurt me. The sudden noise startled me. But it's not like they deliberately hurt me. Just my fussy heart didn't like all the chaos, so they watched me a few days. And they think I hit my head when I fell too. No way to know for sure since I took a little nap as long as I was already lying down." Her familiar smile lifted something in me that I hadn't realized needed lifting. She gave me one last pat and went back to work folding. For her, telling me that much had been a big concession.

"Did you get a look at the robber? Could you tell if it was a man or woman?" She'd said she wouldn't talk about it, but maybe just a little more. I didn't want to make her relive it. I knew how that felt, to relive something bad over and over.

"Not really. I wish I had. I heard the loud noise behind me, and it scared me to death. Silly me, I thought it was a gunshot. It must have been the slam of something on the counter. The next thing I knew I woke up and barely remembered what happened. There's something I'm trying to remember, but I just can't quite get it."

"Why do you think they robbed *you*, Gran?"

"Everybody knows that I'm not too quick to put my money in the bank. I don't make any big secret about that." She shook her head and tucked another stray hair behind her ear. Her naturally curly hair drove her crazy, but she hated to restrain it, calling it God's special blessing. I'd seen pictures of her younger self, and it was a blessing, unlike my cowlicks from Dad.

"I wish you could remember something. Something that would help us find the idiot who sent you to the hospital."

"I don't know, baby girl. Maybe this person needed the money more than I do. I have food. I have a home. We never know what makes people do things."

"I want them caught. They scared you. They took your money and left you on the floor. You could've died and left me, like. . ." I couldn't finish. Some thoughts aren't meant to breathe air.

"Some things happen on this earth that are more than we can ever understand. Remember when I taught you that. After your Momma was taken from us much too soon. We can never understand such things. They aren't ours to know."

That wasn't good enough for me. I slapped the table. "I don't want to hear that. I need to understand some things. It's not fair!" My outburst exploded like a shaken bottle of pop opened too soon.

The front door slammed as two men walked in, distracting me from my shock at slapping the table like that. Gran jumped in her seat, clearly still startled by loud noises. Walter and his friend, Nick-Panda, chose a table across the room with their backs to us. They didn't greet anybody, just stormed to the table, sat down, and argued, with frowns and choppy hands. Not typical small-town public behavior.

The waitress served them two waters and took their orders. As soon as she walked away, they resumed arguing. Panda drew something on a paper. Walter glanced at it, shook his head no, and crumpled up the paper.

Panda's angry voice carried. "You owe me." He rose in his seat, raised a clenched fist, like he would soon throw a punch.

Gran turned a puzzled look toward them. "Such rudeness I won't have here." As she started to get up, Walter threw several twenties on the table and stormed out. They hadn't been served their food yet. Panda followed him. They still hadn't noticed I sat with Gran in a corner of the restaurant.

A little later, Dad came in the door to pick me up. He kissed Gran's cheek but didn't sit down.

"Pick up your pizza at the register, son. I'm covering the dinner shift here tonight, but I know you guys won't mind a pizza." Gran looked away when she said that, like she didn't want to make eye contact. Was she lying? Had I upset her?

We left with pizza for our family dinner, where we'd enjoy it Gran's way, with silver and cloth napkins. It would still taste delicious to bite into the pepperoni with extra cheese! Gran had seemed a little distracted before we left, but I guessed she was still upset by Walter and Panda. I didn't want to admit she might have been upset by my slamming the table.

On the way out, I snatched the paper Walter had crumpled up and left on the table. Inside the car, I unfolded it. Weird. A Halloween doodle of a bunch of headstones. How did this Halloween doodle by Panda make Walter angry enough to shout? What did he owe that rude man anyway?

CHAPTER NINETEEN

Finally! Harlan and I wandered into the cemetery. Max ran straight to Momma and sniffed around her plot before he settled. Max knew our routine.

"Thank goodness your dad offered me some work today." Harlan put the flowers at Momma's grave. "Dad's gotten weird about letting me come over unless there's work involved. I said something to your dad. He's going to start giving me more work."

"That's great, Harlan. You know you could come live with us—"

"That will never happen. It's fine. I just need to be careful. Not get in Dad's way. Best when I'm as invisible as a spirit."

For Harlan to say that much was a big deal. I played it cool.

I examined Momma's spot to be sure I didn't miss some small sign, maybe a feather or something. That butterfly we saw on the way home the other day appearing here would be major. Nothing. Harlan fiddled around with the flowers until he nodded and seemed pleased with the way they looked. I wondered how Momma would ask this delicate question.

"Do you want to talk about home?"

"Nah, talking doesn't do any good. It's okay. He's gone or drunk most of the time anyway." Harlan wiggled his shoulders around like he was loosening them up.

That was the most Harlan had *ever* shared. I had to do this right, and not scare him away from talking. Momma had helped put the right words into my heart.

"You always listen to me. Seems like I oughta do the same," I looked up at him out of the corner of my eye and saw his eyes glaze for a second. When he didn't answer, I pointed to

Zeb's grave, not wanting to push him away, and figured changing the subject might be best. He'd said as much as he planned to, probably more.

"What in the world! We must have moles back here for sure." Harlan smoothed out the dirt and grass around Zeb's tombstone. This was the third or fourth time the dirt and grass had been a mess.

We had gotten permission to do more filming at the cemetery as cover to finally visit and check the cameras. Dad would wonder why we kept staying so long at the graveyard if we weren't using it as the backdrop for our YouTube videos—a perfect collision of filming about spirits and filming spirits. The last thing I needed was to make him think I sat by Momma's grave for hours at a time. His alarms would go off. And I was afraid to talk to him about spirits at all. For now, anyway.

To keep it honest, we set up to film a follow-up to the last cemetery episode for our followers. They were getting impatient and needed a hook to reel them in for Zeb's video, whenever we finally got one. We'd already done a big study of the Highgate Cemetery in London, England, and reported about the search for the Highgate Vampire that people talked about in the 1970s.

But I was certain that Zeb was our treasure. The YouTube sensation that everyone would talk about when we finally captured him on film.

Harlan couldn't take his eyes off the camera hanging on the bus, ready for us. Even while he taped me for YouTube, he kept glancing at the bus. It took all of our willpower to get the video finished first. I added:

We need your inspiration to keep going here. CHALLENGE: This week tell us your most haunting experiences. Maybe a spooky house on Halloween. Maybe a visit to a cemetery. Maybe you stood in line at the grocery and felt someone in line behind you, but no one was there. Tell us all about it. Then tell us what you think makes spirits appear.

Once we finished it and posted a teaser for the ongoing series on Zeb, we hurried to the bus. Harlan took the camera down and we settled in with Max at our feet. We had his water this time, so he slurped away before he settled in. His slurping brought us back to Earth, reminding us that there was more to enjoy than just spirits. We both gave Max a few pats before diving in.

We huddled over the camera. We thought we had nothing. . . until suddenly we had *something*. My pulse raced. Harlan nearly dropped the camera. Max sensed our excitement and tried to butt his head in between us as we watched the footage on the spirit camera. Time stamped Saturday, yesterday, a figure appeared right by Zebediah's tombstone. We froze the frame for a minute, and then rewatched the image again and again. We'd dreamt of capturing a spirit, but *this*, what we saw instead took our breath away, and puzzled us more than any spirit could have. It was a clue to our other puzzle and possibly more important than a spirit. At least for now.

"That's no spirit. Look, that's our logo, our armor vest. That's a paintball customer." Harlan's excited voice couldn't have been happier if we'd scored a spirit.

"And a big man. Look at those shoulders. But what's he doing?" I asked, freezing the frame again. Why would a paintball customer be inside the high fence of the cemetery? It's not like he could be there accidentally, since that area was fenced in. And the paintball games that Saturday had been clear across the property in a different popular gaming area, the old junkyard.

We replayed that part of the clip several times. These cameras weren't made to take clear images like a photo, so it was grainy, like you see on the news when a Quik-Mart films a suspect with those mounted cameras.

Something lingered in my memory, just out of reach. I closed my eyes, asked Zeb for help. Finally, a flash of another scene played in my head.

"That's it! That's why that figure looks familiar! It's just like the one on the news. The robbery at Dairy Queen. Same size figure, same way of stooping over." My heart beat fast with excitement that we could catch the guy who caused Gran to collapse. At the same time my mind filled with the disappointment that it hadn't been Zeb we caught on film. I'd hoped to be one step closer to knowing how to communicate with Momma. Instead, we'd caught something else.

"Look close, Scooter. Look what he's doing." Harlan's voice shook with excitement. We scrunched around the camera again, Max in the middle.

On screen, the big figure had a tool in his hand, maybe a little shovel. He knelt near the headstone and flung dirt out of a hole. We had to rewind several times, until it became clear to us that this person had *buried* something in the ground over Zeb's grave, very close to the weathered ancient tombstone. Since the camera focus had included Zeb's headstone, this person showed fully in the video! Was this what Zeb had tried to tell me about? Someone using his sacred ground for a loot locker? No wonder he'd been so fired up. Desecration of a grave showed serious disrespect. I'd hoped Zeb was telling me something from Momma, but I guessed now that this was the reason for his unrest.

"Can you tell who it is?" I asked Harlan.

"No, not really. But I think we can put the pieces together—robberies, Zeb angry, familiar robber figure burying stuff in secret. At least that size would have cleared Gran for sure, if she hadn't been cleared already by getting robbed. This guy is lots bigger than her."

"Wait! Let's dig it up. Then we'll know for sure."

"First, with what? But more important, have you ever watched a crime movie? You can't disturb the evidence if you want the criminal convicted." Harlan's logic slowed me down. I wanted this creep convicted.

"Then we can't tell anybody," I said. "We're

not sure yet. Besides, how would we explain all this to anybody? To Dad? They'd never believe two kids anyway." My heart pumped like I'd already been caught doing something Dad would be disappointed about.

"You did finally tell him about the camera, right?" Harlan glared at me, then shook his head when I didn't answer right away.

"Not exactly." My stomach dropped. "I said I would eventually, and I tried, twice." I explained what had happened.

I had to figure out how to make it okay about the camera. Dad wouldn't like me spending $400 of my savings for it without his permission. Especially from an all-sales-final Internet site, and especially to tape spirits. No matter how hard I might try to explain about spirits, he still didn't believe like I did—like Momma had. And after she died, he didn't even want to talk about afterlife. He clearly didn't get the family gift I got—the one that let me understand hauntings. That came from Momma. Especially with these robberies going on, he didn't want to hear about a spirit camera. Somehow, I needed to be able to help him see it was now a robber camera too.

"This is a great time to tell me all that!" Harlan

whipped away from me. But before he did, he turned those dark eyes of his into daggers. He didn't often look at me like that.

Tears spilled. I couldn't help it. Max jumped up, confused by the atmosphere since he's a "sensitive" and all. I buried my head in his fur, hoping to hide my tears. I couldn't say anything at first. Eventually, I managed a feeble sorry. It went unanswered.

The trek back to the house passed in silence. Harlan's footsteps pounded the pavement in front of me. Even Max abandoned me and trotted beside Harlan. I could've caught up, but I got his message. I guess my truth rubber band had stretched too tight and snapped. I hoped our friendship hadn't.

When we got back to the house, I said I was sick and went to my room for a while. Harlan would be fine with Dad and Uncle Ezra until dinner. He'd rather be with them than me right now anyway. I needed a few minutes to get past the anger and disappointment in my best friend's muddy eyes.

Now here we were with evidence to show a robber burying loot in our cemetery, and it was my own fault we couldn't take it straight to Dad. The same robber who hurt Gran. The robber I needed to put away.

The only way we could share it would get me in deep trouble. There had to be a way to fix this.

CHAPTER TWENTY

I joined the family in the kitchen. They were deep in conversation when I rolled in. Even the smell of the fried chicken already on the table didn't lift my spirits. Gran went all out today.

Gran turned quizzical eyes on me—I'd splashed water to hide that I'd been crying, but she never missed much.

"Harlan, we ever tell you about the time we drove our old tractor into the lake?" Dad grinned at Uncle Ezra. Seems like when Harlan visited, they especially enjoyed tormenting Gran with reminders of the crazy things they'd done as young teens. Or, maybe they wanted to loosen Harlan up. He didn't seem to have much fun in his life.

"You boys should be ashamed to admit to that lie. You didn't tell the truth until you were twenty-five. I blamed that poor neighbor boy, Billy, all those years. Never let him come around after that."

"Tell me about the old drive-in. How did you sneak in?" Harlan asked.

"Dad had some good wire clippers," Uncle Ezra said. He grinned at Dad. "Of course, times were different. You'd get in trouble nowadays. Back then, they made us work it off. One whole summer of free labor."

"That fence never did all stay mended at the same time. Gran baked us cookies every time because she thought we had club meetings. It was a club, sort of. Until we got caught one too many times."

Their favorite story was about the party they threw when Gran and Gramps went to Branson, Missouri, to see her favorite performers, and they sent the babysitter on a wild goose chase for the night. Harlan had probably heard that one ten times, and still smiled like it was the first time he'd ever heard it.

Even though Harlan stayed for dinner, he avoided speaking to me as much as possible. I didn't blame him. He had every right to be upset, but I'd be sadder than saddest if he stayed mad long. I hadn't lied outright, just used the truth continuum to my advantage. Everything we said was somewhere on that continuum—from mirror image of exact truth, to a little twist on the way we see it, to an outright bold-faced lie that deserves some time in your friend's cold zone.

With all the laughter, you'd think it was a fun dinner, but not for me. I'd let Harlan down. I hated for him to be mad at me. I didn't want to lose him. And I couldn't let Gran's robber go free for one more day. What if he hurt someone else? Food sat like bricks at the pit of my stomach. Sometimes I didn't think slow-down-and-think was a flower that grew in my garden.

After dinner, Harlan and I went to my room.

"All right, so those still pictures of the figure at the cemetery I took with my phone, maybe they'll help. I'll fool around with some editing tools tonight and see if I can make anything a little clearer." He showed me at least twenty shots on his phone. Thank goodness he thought to do that. What if we somehow lost what was on the video? What would happen then? I was lucky to have Harlan.

"Are you still mad?" I needed to know exactly where he stood. I knew he'd have a tough time staying mad while he was petting Max, the best peacemaker in all of the world. He'd been petting Max since we got to my room. Max knew how to make everybody love him, and hopefully by extension, me too.

"No, but if you want to be partners, don't get me in trouble with your dad. That's a deal breaker. You know how much I respect him." Max almost purred at Harlan's softer tone and nuzzled his head against him to remind Harlan of his job petting him. As much as a huge dog can purr, Max kept up his display of happiness, and tapped Harlan's hand any time he quit.

The boulder and bricks had completely lifted when Harlan said he wasn't mad anymore, and now something tight in my chest opened when he smiled his regular smile. I took a deep breath. I couldn't remember a time when Harlan had cold-shouldered me like he did today. But Harlan loved my family about as much as he loved me, so I'd best be keeping that in mind. Ain't no education in the second kick of a mule—I wasn't looking for any more psychic kicks from my best friend.

"So, what's next? I don't know what to do," I said, wanting these worries about robberies to be gone so I could concentrate on the spirits, on Momma's spirit. But we needed to get busy and find Gran's robber and get him in jail. What if he came to paintball?

"Slow down, Scooter. We aren't gonna solve anything tonight. Let me see what I can see in the pictures, and then we'll decide. I think we'll have some proof, and we'll get help from the adults. It's time. We'll figure out how." Max finally let Harlan have a rest and flounced onto my bed for a quick snooze.

"At least it's good to be able to prove it was a man, a man who comes to paintball. If we can't share the pictures, we have to figure out how to catch this creep who's using our cemetery." I wanted it done now.

"Right now, let's slow it down, and see what we have first." Harlan would do the best he could to get pictures clear enough that we could use. And fast.

Harlan copied the time line I'd done for the robberies we knew about. He'd find a way to get more information from his uncle without giving away our investigation. His uncle knew everybody and everything going on for miles around ever since he started in real estate. He said it was all about networking, so he networked the heck out of everybody.

Harlan and I went back to join the family for a while. Gran smiled and nodded at me, like she could tell we'd made our peace. She might not be Momma's mother, but she had some kind of mountain mind-reading gift of her own. Lots of folks in the hills had special gifts.

We all hung around and listened to Dad and Uncle Ezra strum a few tunes on their guitars on the front porch. Fireflies twinkled in the fields, and the moonless night hid the grounds. Tree frogs and crickets played their own tunes. Harlan's uncle arrived to pick him up at eight, but hung with us on the porch for a while before they left. He grabbed his fiddle from his car, and we enjoyed an old-fashioned mountain porch party.

It was a perfect night for a haunting. But no spirits visited. When Dad strummed one of Momma's favorite songs though, I could picture her face, and that was a sort of spirit visit, I think. I touched where Momma's necklace used to be—the spot warmed my fingers.

CHAPTER TWENTY-ONE

Harlan paced back and forth as soon as he saw me, too cool to show his excitement openly, but not able to hold it in. It took forever to get to him. Max must have sensed my eagerness because he raced ahead of me. Harlan had snuck out for a weekday visit while his dad was at work. He'd waited on the front porch when he beat Uncle Ezra and me home from the doctor.

"You guys coming in for some of my outer space pasta?" Uncle Ezra sounded pretty proud about his lunch plans.

My belly growled, but Harlan's wide eyes signaled me to see what he had to say first.

"We'll be in soon." Outer space pasta? Only Uncle Ezra.

After Uncle Ezra went in, Harlan said, "You won't believe what we caught on tape!" His excited voice carried, and he lowered it when he realized how loudly he'd spoken.

"Don't keep me waiting. Spill!" As excited as he sounded, it had to be something big.

"First, it's definitely a paintball customer. The vest was visible, and it was the rental stuff that you and I hand out. It was too fuzzy to make out much, but I'm sure it was one of our vests—the logo is clear enough to tell that. That narrows it down to people who were there that Saturday and rented our stuff."

"First? There's more?" I asked. A narrowed field of suspects sounded promising. The liability waivers might have the name, assuming someone used their real name. After all, this guy had been pretty smart so far, at least about not getting caught.

"Second, looking at the person's size, the figure is clearly adult male. We didn't have any teens or women that Saturday big enough to match." His excited look told me he'd saved the best for last.

I didn't let him suffer. "Please tell me the third."

"Third, you could see him pull bills from a money bag, then put that into a box, like a little cashbox, the kind Gran kept under the counter. Like the one that went missing in her robbery, I bet."

"Wow! You got all that from your pictures?" His skill with photo editing impressed me—I'd seen the fuzzy shots he'd started with.

"Yeah. What I didn't get was any sleep last night. I had to tinker with the shots all night trying to make sense of it all and trying to get clear enough pictures that we could share with Critter."

Those last words gut-punched me. Harlan had a plan that included Critter.

By then, we needed to make an appearance for lunch. It was only Uncle Ezra and us today, so it was a perfect chance to ask him some questions.

"Any news on Gran's robbery?" I was dying to tell him what we knew about a paintball customer burying loot on our property. But Dad had the right to know first.

"No, but there's been another one. The guy they suspected had been doing them was drying out in jail when this one went down, so it couldn't have been him. Though they said the new one could be a copycat." Uncle Ezra passed the pasta, like that news wasn't the most important thing going on in our holler.

Where in the world did he find pasta shaped like tiny rockets? And the cheese sauce! It was delicious.

"Where was it?" Harlan asked.

"Right down the street, Saturday morning, at Harding's Hardware."

I dropped my fork. The clatter made Max howl. Harlan shot a warning glance my way. Should I tell Uncle Ezra and take my chances? As if he read my mind, Harlan shook his head no.

Uncle Ezra had made my favorite banana pudding, the kind with cookies and pudding and meringue. Yummy! When he left the kitchen for a few minutes I could barely contain myself.

"Are you thinking what I'm thinking?" I asked.

"Well, yeah. That tape was a fresh robbery.

That guy has nerve, robbing and burying on the same day. Wonder if he always does that?"

"Probably not since we usually use that field on Saturdays. But we were on the other field so far away, I guess he got brave. Not that robbing anybody is brave."

Uncle Ezra popped back into the kitchen, "I'm sure you guys have some videos to make. I'll do the cleanup today."

So we skedaddled out of there.

Harlan and I booted up the computer. We found the headline: ANOTHER LOCAL ROBBERY: CASH DRAWER EMPTIED AT HARDING'S HARDWARE, but there weren't any more details than we already knew.

"You have to tell your dad." Harlan scowled and, even while petting Max, his jaw tightened.

"Just give me a little bit longer. We have to think this through." I had a lot to think about. I didn't want Dad mad at me, but especially not at Harlan. If Dad got upset with Harlan, it might crush him, and we were all Harlan had besides his uncle. We were his family. And, I didn't quite trust Critter after he'd arrested Gran.

We needed a break while we thought over

our options, so we worked on the video Uncle Ezra had mentioned. Time for a YouTube update if we wanted to keep our viewers hooked. We had to be ready for whatever happened next on film—spirit or robber.

"Look, spirit_talk suggested that we camp overnight at Zeb's site. Wonder if we could do that?"

Harlan looked at me like I had two heads.

"Oh, yeah, guess we better find the robber first. I'll just say that we'll definitely plan on doing that soon."

"Spookster101 wants live pictures of the inside of Sun Valley. As soon as we can, we need to see if Uncle Ezra will get us out there again. Oh, maybe we should make that our lead in October. They'll be starting their haunted tours then."

"Yeah, go ahead and answer that we'll do the tour and share photos. We can use the new camera. It won't be hard to get it off the mount."

Caught up with our responses, I pulled up the information about Swan Pond, the church and cemetery in Tennessee that I'd been researching.

"How about this one for our next post? It's a

cemetery, so a great lead-in to more on Zeb, or whatever happens in our cemetery?"

"That's cool! Sure, but I hope we have something live to show from our camera soon, something ghostly." Harlan stroked Max and knotted his brows, clearly not into Swan Pond.

When I shut the computer down, he must have realized he'd hurt my feelings.

"That's close enough we might be able to go to it soon," Harlan answered, eager for a field trip, and trying to make up for being distracted. "Have you read all these comments on haunting experiences? Wow! We're not the only ones who believe!"

"How do you think we got so many followers? Of course, other people want to know about spirits."

Harlan gave me one of those looks he's so good at, like *get over yourself*.

"Okay, enough of that. How can we help Momma show herself? That's the spirit I want to know about right now. And what are we going to do about catching this robber before he hits paintball?"

CHAPTER TWENTY-TWO

Saturday finally rolled around again. Harlan slung a few of the familiar vests with our logo over to my area, getting ready for the onslaught.

"I still think we should talk to Critter about this." Harlan's brows furrowed in worry.

"I promise. Just let's try this and see what happens. Then we'll tell." I wanted to try my plan first, and then we'd talk to Critter. I questioned his judgment—after all, he'd arrested Gran. He should have known better, no matter what it looked like. Just because a pig has curls like a sheep, that doesn't mean he's a sheep.

We'd be in so much trouble if Dad found out about what we planned to do today because it involved the business, but only the guilty person would react, so it wasn't like it would be bad for the business. We had to take the chance. It wasn't a surefire plan, but at least we'd be doing something, which beat doing nothing. And Dad had specifically told me that the robberies took precedence over the spirits.

Everybody bought paint at our window, so all the players today should see our sign: Due to excavation of some areas of the cemetery the fields around O.K. Corral will be closed next week.

Our fake notice should send someone scurrying to dig up their loot before the excavation. Since we had caught them on tape before, we hoped we could do it again. It wasn't foolproof, but it was worth a try. I thought it could work—Harlan wasn't sure people would even notice the sign but had let me talk him into it. He at least expected it was harmless if it failed.

Suddenly we were slammed. A few players glanced at the sign but didn't seem to pay much attention to what it said.

Creepy Pete stood in front of the sign, moved his lips as he read it to himself, then said, "It don't seem right to do that around a cemetery." As he walked away, he made a quick phone call. That was strange. I'd never once seen him use a phone.

"Hey, can I drive the dig machine? Are you guys adding some more buildings?" one of our regulars asked.

Right behind him stood Nick-Panda, who asked, "Yeah, what are you building?"

"I'm not sure exactly what's going on," Harlan answered, while I ducked down as if I'd dropped something to avoid answering. Made more sense for Harlan not to know something like that.

The sign got more attention than we expected. It was a good thing no one but Harlan and I heard all the questions. Dad and Uncle Ezra might have blown a gasket. It would have taken a lot of explaining. They worked far enough away from us that, as long as we stayed on the lookout, they would never see the sign.

Dad had left earlier to take his money to the house. We'd finished passing out paint to the last few stragglers. Everyone waited in the staging area for Dad and Uncle Ezra to let them onto the fields. Harlan and I had been so preoccupied with watching reactions to our sign that we hadn't noticed that Dad had been gone longer than normal. The side door opened, and Dad rushed in, looking frantic. He ran behind the counter and dug through things like a mother in search of a pacifier for a screaming baby in church. His hair stood on end and he kept shaking his head and muttering.

Max, who'd followed Dad back in, rushed over to him like he sensed Dad needed help. Usually he returned to me as soon as they got back. Harlan and I stared. We'd never seen Dad so hectically search for anything in the store. He loved to brag about his wild old days, but he'd settled into being a dad very calmly. And he never let me see him sweat, saying kids shouldn't have to deal with grown-up problems, and it was a shame when they had to. Cool, calm, and collected—usually.

"It's gone!" He squeezed his scalp and looked around with dazed eyes.

"What? What's gone?" I yelled from across the room. Seeing him like this scared me to death. My stomach dropped. I touched my neck—no necklace.

"Last week's take. Over $2,000. When I went to put today's money away, the cashbox was empty. It was there, but it was empty. I was hoping I'd left it here."

"But, Dad, last week's would already be in the. . ." I could tell by his ghostly grimace that he hadn't made it to the bank. "Oh, no."

He collapsed in a heap in a chair. Uncle Ezra came back in from the staging area, where he'd been waiting for Dad so they could start the games. He took one look at Dad and rushed to his side. "Is it Mom?" he asked.

"No. No. Go back out there and get them started by yourself. I'll explain later."

Uncle Ezra hesitated, but he had a group of impatient customers waiting. In their silent twin exchange, he made sure that was what Dad wanted him to do, and then headed out.

By then, I'd rolled over to Dad, and hugged him from the side. Harlan read my mind and gave us a minute alone.

"It'll be okay, Dad." I didn't know what else to say. Dad never, ever talked to me about money, but I knew money was tight. Everything had changed after Momma died, so it only made sense that our money changed too. My bills for treatment cost a lot. I saw him with piles of medical bills, shuffling through them. I heard him make payment plans at doctors' offices, even though he whispered to the people who took care of that. This might mean disaster for our property. Two weeks of cash, and Gran's losses too.

"The worst part is that it's probably a regular, someone who's seen our pattern on Saturdays." Dad's eyes closed for a second and his shoulders slumped. I expected that hurt him way more than the money did. Mountain trust is as true to the hills as corn bread.

Wheels spun in my head like a hamster turning while I calculated whether to tell Dad what Harlan and I knew, right here, right now. We were too late to stop this robbery, and I could kick myself for not moving faster. What good would it do now to tell him what we knew when we didn't have answers yet? If we waited and followed our plan, we might get Dad's money back since it probably wasn't buried yet. Relief flooded me that Dad hadn't been hurt. If I hadn't already been sitting down, I'd have needed to as a sudden flood of shakiness almost floored me. Something truly awful might have happened today. Could I have prevented it?

This robber definitely had some complications now, assuming he saw our sign about the cemetery excavation. More money, our *money*, to hide and the need to move what he had already hidden in the cemetery. If I waited this out, and caught the thieving creep burying this money, I might be able to get our money back. The pressure to get the money buried fast might make him do something stupid. I hoped it wasn't the pressure from our sign that made him rob Dad to begin with, but I doubted that. This had probably been planned for a while. He'd probably watched us for a long time to figure out the perfect timing for hitting either our house or wherever Dad kept the money. It might've happened any time this week for all I knew. This guy seemed like a big planner, hitting places with easy money, quick cash, and trusting small-town hearts. The way the robberies had been spaced out, I'd thought we had more time before another robbery. Seemed like he was getting careless, hitting so many so near each other and so fast.

When Critter showed up to take a statement, Dad took him over to the house to talk, which made sense. He wouldn't want to upset his customers, but mostly, I think he didn't want to upset Harlan and me. I dreaded more than ever disappointing him when he found out what we'd been up to. I had to deliver good evidence along with our explanation. I was in pretty deep, and I'd dragged Harlan with me. All I'd wanted was to find Momma's spirit, and instead I'd found the monster who hurt Gran, and now had robbed Dad. How could I have expected spirits *and* robbers at paintball? When I got my hands on that robber, I was fixin' to jerk a knot in his tail. He'd be sorry he ever tangled with Chamber's Creek.

Somehow, we got through that day. I almost found Critter and talked to him before he left, but I wanted one more day, just one more day. Harlan worked like a robot, worried sick about it all.

Gran came back early and fixed dinner at home for us. This dinner didn't fit our usual pattern of chaos and fun. Gran patted Max herself, and fed him scraps, as if even she needed comfort from his warmth today.

Gran did my bedtime routine. I missed Dad.

I missed Momma.

CHAPTER TWENTY-THREE

I lay in bed wide awake, missing Dad, knowing how upset he must have been to skip tucking me in. He hadn't missed many nights since Momma went to heaven, and never without an explanation. This must be a money disaster for us. I glanced at Yoda, but for once none of his words filled my heart.

My soul twisted in a way that wasn't very becoming to a Southern girl. I wanted to rip that no-good robber's head off and feed it to some hogs. First Gran, now Dad.

I needed a surefire way to catch this good-for-nothing thief who'd crushed my daddy. It was too late to undo whatever our sign had triggered, so tomorrow we might be lucky enough to find proof with new film, and then we'd get help.

The robber wouldn't be able to get into the cemetery easily tomorrow—we were counting on that. The high fence made it accessible only from one gate. There was a clear view of that gate from the house.

Since Gran had come to stay, we went to eleven o'clock services, then out to lunch, rain or shine. So, we typically were gone for several hours at that time every Sunday. I counted on the thief knowing our habits and digging up his loot at that exact time. Nighttime would be too risky because a flashlight would be easy to see from the house.

Lying awake, at around 2 a.m., I texted Harlan.

I have a plan. We're going to catch this thief in person. Failproof. Not just depend on the camera.

He answered right away. At 2 a.m., as soon as he got my text. He loved Dad, maybe he lay awake worried too.

Okay. Spill.

I'm going to be too sick to go to church tomorrow. We need answers. And not from God.

I think it's time to get help. Like, from Critter.

If this doesn't work, we will. Promise. Be here by 11.

I'll be there. But I think it's wrong.

Then don't do it.

Not letting you do it alone. Whatever IT is. I'll be there.

K. Be here BY 11. Bring a good camera. We'll have to hurry.

***

As soon as everybody left for church, Harlan snuck up the driveway. I didn't ask how he'd managed to get a ride over during peak church-going time. We had to get busy.

"I took the bus keys." I dangled the keys in front of Harlan's startled face. They'd been hanging on a key rack unmoved for ages.

"You what? Have you lost your mind?"

"Not to drive it, you idiot. We can hide on it and see the cemetery from the windows. We'll catch them in the act. There'll be film and eyewitnesses. And pictures." I pointed at his camera.

"I don't think that's a very good idea," Harlan said in slow motion, like I couldn't understand words or was hard of hearing. "It's time to turn this over. Now. Let's call Uncle Ezra and get him here. Or Critter. We can leave your dad out of it for now."

"It's perfect. That man crushed Dad." I took off and Harlan and Max followed. "We need to take care of this now!" No one had passed the house yet, but we might not have much time to start up the bus without anybody hearing it.

When we got to the bus, Harlan tried again to talk me out of getting on it.

"It's too hot for you to be sitting on that bus." Harlan pointed to the sun glinting off the bus roof. The bus had no air conditioning, one of the main reasons it had been junked and became part of the paintball park's game grounds. Today it sported even more colorful paint splatters because it hadn't rained in a while. Most of the windows were covered in paint, favorite target practice for aim—the glass was shatterproof, and one of Dad's rules was about how close you could stand for target practice.

"We won't be on it that long. Go on up there and start the engine. We have to get that engine off before anybody hears it. Hopefully, the lift will work today."

While we worked on getting me on board with the lift, the skitter of squirrels nearby attracted Max's attention and he dashed off to play chase. I didn't want him messing up our surveillance, so I called him back after a while, and got him settled down. I wished I'd brought him some water because he was panting already. If I let him loose, he could grab some water at the creek, but I didn't want him running around anymore, or wandering off.

Once Zoomster, Max, Harlan, and I were all aboard, we settled in to watch the cemetery. With the windows covered by paint splatter, we only had peepholes. Even if we'd wanted to open a window, they were rusted shut after sitting out here so long.

We turned on the old battery-operated portable cassette player really low and played country tunes while we waited for something to happen. I was pretty sure they'd taken the bait about the cemetery excavation, and would dig up their loot in a panic, especially after watching Creepy Pete make a phone call as soon as he saw the sign. Wonder who he'd been calling to alert.

Creepy Pete might have a nice nephew, but my gut said he might be a robber in his spare time. He'd been the only one to have suspicious behavior when he saw the sign. He'd stood back and read it over and over, scrunching his brows like he was deep in thought before moving on, then made that phone call.

After a while Harlan got edgy. "Let's call this off, Scooter. You're dripping, Max is panting, and I'm sitting in a puddle of sweat."

Then, everything seemed to happen at once.

I pointed toward the woods. "Shhh! Look!"

Harlan turned the music off. "Wait. What?"

Instead of men with shovels moving toward the cemetery, men gathered in the woods. At least three men moved through the thick woods—it was hard to count. We were too far away to recognize them, and they were all in full camouflage, so it would be impossible even if we were closer. A tall head showed in front of a maple, a slightly shorter figure a few trees away. The short one looked suspiciously like

Creepy Pete, just as I thought. But why were there three of them? They moved separately, far apart.

"They're gone."

"Wait. Look again."

It seemed like three different people, but it might've been only two. I tried to track all of the figures, but the woods and brush made it impossible. I twisted my stringy hair into a tight pony, like that would help me see better. If only.

We hadn't expected three. Two wouldn't have surprised us too much. But, three?

"What's going on?" I asked Harlan. "Can you tell how many are out there? Seems like three to me, and one looks like Creepy Pete. I knew it was him."

"I'm not sure. They keep moving," Harlan said. "Seems like they're tracking someone the way they keep ducking around trees. Or hiding from each other. I can't tell what's going on. This is crazy!"

"Oh, no. We'd better get out of here." I rolled my chair onto the lift platform. Even I understood that we didn't stand a chance against three grown men if we were on this bus. Sweat trickled down my neck, and internal alarms clanged. What had I gone and gotten us into? If we got off now, maybe they wouldn't see us on that side of the bus. If we stayed, they might come for us.

My phone lay on my bedside table at the house. But Harlan always carried his. As soon as we got off the bus, he could call Critter. We'd bypass Uncle Ezra—this situation needed the law. Right now, we'd better concentrate on getting off this bus though. Fast!

Some distance stood between us and the men. The lift door was on the opposite side of the bus from where they were prowling among the trees. If we left right now, maybe they wouldn't see or hear us, and we could get help. Even though we didn't understand for sure *what* was going on, three men shouldn't be wandering in our woods. One of those guys was the robber who'd hurt Gran—and he might hurt someone else.

The roar of the motor when Harlan started the bus to lower the lift must have echoed for miles. I flinched. We exchanged looks. Even when I got used to the noise of the running engine, I prayed for us to be able to shut it off soon. Harlan tried to engage the lift mechanism. Nothing. He tried again. Again nothing. Harlan swore a word I'd never heard him use. Gran would've made us both eat soap.

One of the men, the tall one, seemed to be heading toward the bus in a zigzag pattern. I swore the same word Harlan had just used and prayed my stomach would stop curdling. Harlan switched off the ignition, turned to me, and blinked his big brown eyes, like a curious owl. *What now?*

CHAPTER TWENTY-FOUR

"Call Critter. Now!" I knew we didn't have much time if that guy continued to head our way.

Harlan reached for his pocket. He stared, a blank look in his eyes. "I left the house in a hurry. I don't have my phone. You call."

My look told him everything he needed to know.

"Harlan, I think you could slip out and run home down by the lake. You need to get out while you can. You can bring help back for me."

No need for both of us to be stuck here. Our predicament was all my fault. I had no business on this bus, and I knew it.

"No way I'm leaving you here alone. Someone at home will miss us when they get back from church. Someone will come." He dug his fingers into his tight cap of black curls, knelt down, and turned his eyes to mine. "No way in hell."

As determined and strong as he had been that first day I met him in elementary school. The best friend a girl could have. Right now, a little less determined and strong might have been safer for him.

I caught another glimpse of camouflage at the edge of the woods. My heart pounded. My mind raced. My stomach heaved. Max put his head on my knee. Then nothing. Relief flooded through me, and I shook out my hands that I'd been clenching. Until I saw another flash of camouflage.

We sat in the silence, both patting Max. The heat curled around us like blazes of a place I never want to visit. Every noise sounded off. Birds chirped, but not like normal. When Harlan shifted his weight and the seat squeaked, I ducked.

"Men shouldn't be tracking through here on a Sunday morning," Harlan whispered. I nodded.

All thought of capturing a thief had left right about the time we saw those three men—that made it real. I'd pulled not only myself, but my best friend right alongside me, into a situation "beyond our pay grade," as Dad liked to say. Not to mention the poor, thirsty dog trembling at my feet. All I'd wanted was to connect with Momma, not trip across a stash of loot in our cemetery.

Our position, trapped inside the bus without a way to contact anybody, meant we were stuck here. Critter, in his full deputy-on-duty getup, would be the best sight ever right now. Fact was, I'd never seen an officer of the law *on* the paintball fields. In the offices, yes, but never on the fields.

And then the figures appeared again, but closer to the edge of the woods. They were bound to notice the bus. Connect the sound they'd heard to the bus starting up.

As terrified as I was, I still imagined us capturing those guys. But what chance did two kids have against three men?

"Okay, paintball queen, what do we do now? Three is a little more than we bargained for." Harlan tried to put some kidding tone into his voice, but it didn't work. Sweat ran down his cheeks, or they could have been tears. His wide eyes probably mirrored my own.

I'd been imagining Blake Shelton's soft crooning. I loved Blake, but his crooning wasn't right for this nightmare. This had more of a Johnny Cash vibe—darkness and regrets.

I gave Harlan my version of the evil eye. "I don't know. If Dad was mad about the camera, what do you think he'd say about this?" We couldn't tell where the guys were now. They'd disappeared again. They'd do that. But reappear somewhere else.

My mind raced like a hound chasing a rabbit. Beside me, Max cowered and whined, looking up at me with brown eyes that said *I'm sorry*.

No one at home knew we were hunkered down in the bus in this heat. Dad and Uncle Ezra wouldn't know to rescue us here. They'd never in a million years expect us to get on this bus. They'd be in the woods, in the direct path of the robbers if they did come looking for us. Of all days for both of us to be without our phones.

Then Max suddenly loosed an eerie, wolfish howl. My skin crawled, like a million beetles covered me. I had no idea what triggered that howl, unless Zeb had communicated bad news to Max.

Momma, please help us. But neither Zeb nor Momma seemed to come forward—no stir in the air, no flashes, no orbs. Only the flash of movement in the woods.

I should be thinking now about what I'd do when we made it out. If we made it out. Obviously, I needed a plan, and I needed one fast. The only plan my brain mustered involved Harlan leaving me behind, which he still refused to do. Maybe we could figure out a way to send Max for help, but by now he was so overheated that he might not make it. Besides, he was channeling the Cowardly Lion of Oz, shaking and whining, and not likely to run to get help even if I *threw* him out.

I poked my head close enough to look out the window at the wooded area to our right. Flashes of movement appeared in the woods, but I couldn't be sure what they were. The robbers were wearing camo, and it worked as advertised—they blended right into the trees. With so many evergreens, plenty of hiding spots remained available. Maybe the men would head away from us. Maybe they weren't after us.

Then a figure from the woods moved toward the bus.

Someone must have seen us peeking out earlier. Crap. Maybe they only wanted to scare us away. Send us running. Except—I couldn't run even if my life depended on it. Max whined on a higher note at my feet, huddled into a roly-poly ball of dark fur. He followed his no-bark command like a trooper, but I wasn't sure how long that would last. I stroked him and wished I'd never trapped him in here with us. He'd have gotten us help long ago if only he could.

Harlan pulled me away from the window. "Why'd you go and show yourself like that? Do you *want* to get us hurt?" Harlan had known better than to let his head be seen, but I'd been stupid enough to be visible to someone out there. I got a better look out. They got a look at me.

Harlan helped me get myself onto the floor beside him. He mimicked Max, making himself as small as possible, not easy since his growth spurt this past year. I wanted to pat his head and calm him down, too, like I had Max, but I was too busy praying and wallowing in my own heat and panic. I moved my lips in a prayer to Momma.

"You, on that bus, come out," a voice boomed, but we saw no one.

The three of us huddled together. A fist pounded the door of the bus.

"Momma, please help us," I prayed out loud.

At that moment, a warmth surrounded me, and suddenly I knew Momma was there. No butterfly, nothing to see, just a feeling. But what a feeling! For the first time since the accident, I *knew* she was with me, absolutely positively for sure. In some strange way, I appreciated this crazy mess I'd gotten us into if that's what it took for me to be with Momma for a moment. My heart slowed, my stalled breathing started up again, my brain opened up, and I knew we'd be okay. However, the peaceful lull soon exploded.

CHAPTER TWENTY-FIVE

Bang, bang, bang! The fist pounded again. "Come out of there or we're coming in."

Birds nested in a nearby tree blasted away in a loud rush of wings. The stink of our sweat and fear would gag a maggot. Poor Max trembled like a hula dancer now. The birds had startled him as much as the banging. If only I could channel some of my peace from Momma to Harlan and Max.

Sirens whooped in the distance—the sound soothed by reminding us that help *could* come. Would it get here fast enough?

Harlan scooted closer on the floor, reached out, held my hand. "We'll be okay, Scooter."

My heart lifted. Maybe Momma's spirit had taken him in too. She'd always loved Harlan, and I knew she appreciated him taking such good care of me.

The quiet lasted a few precious minutes. The person banging seemed to go away. But, where did they go? Who was it? Nobody would pound like that if they were friendly.

I got situated back in my chair. This time I stayed low. Away from the windows. Max's quaking slowed. Harlan hovered close to both of us, keeping himself between me and the window.

Hunkering down and waiting might be our best bet. But the sweat poured off our faces as the bus heated up even more. Air felt like it had actual consistency that had to be swallowed in a gulp. Maybe Harlan would leave now if I convinced him I'd be safe waiting here.

We dared to move to the windows again. To see if all was clear. Before the heat made one of us pass out. Two different figures wove in and out of the woods. It was impossible to keep up with everybody in the woods, but these two wore regular clothes and their builds would've made me believe they were Dad and Uncle Ezra if I hadn't known they were at church.

Five people stalked around our woods. It was impossible to tell what those people knew about the others surrounding them. We had a higher view from up here in the bus. I worried about the new people we'd seen. They might not know there were *three* others. That they were criminals.

Then I caught a glimpse of the blue shirt Dad loved best, from his first concert, on one of the two new people. He stood maybe ten feet away from where I'd last spotted the robber.

"We have to warn him," I whispered to Harlan, and filled my lungs with air, ready to scream.

"No!" Harlan's frantic cry stopped me just in time. "Maybe the guy doesn't know your dad is there. You'll draw attention to him. You could get him hurt. Or worse."

Again, acting without thinking it through. My mind raced with possibilities of what could've happened.

Dad, go home. Please! Just go home!

We must have been trapped longer than it seemed, or they'd still be at church. But when I glanced at my watch, it was pretty early still, and they shouldn't have been home. Time had taken on some kind of warp. Slow became fast, and fast slowed down. Now I'd put Harlan, Dad, and Uncle Ezra in danger. Even Max might get hurt or have heat stroke.

Please, Dad, don't do anything stupid. I closed my eyes and had a few words with God. I'm sorry for skipping church, and lying, I promise never to do any of those things again if you just protect my family and Harlan. I'd lost enough. I did all the right things, tried to be a good person. Except for truth stretching on occasion, and I'd try to do better even with that. He couldn't punish me more. "Momma, time to look after Dad now," I prayed out loud.

The scene in the woods came to life. Sweat— or tears—rolled down my cheeks.

Through our peek hole, Uncle Ezra, the one not in the blue shirt, stood near somebody on the ground at the edge of the woods. Please, God, let Dad be okay. I couldn't see Dad or his blue shirt. Vomit rose in my throat. I prayed that Uncle Ezra hadn't accidentally hurt the brother who'd arrived within minutes of his own entry into this world.

Everything happened all at once, in a blur. Dad burst out of the woods and raced toward the bus. If Dad could run, then who in the world was on the ground at Uncle Ezra's feet? And what was Dad doing running through that open space when someone could have a gun? I couldn't bear it—I closed my eyes tight.

What if Dad got hurt running to the bus? It would be all my fault, and I wouldn't get to tell him goodbye either. I closed my eyes. I couldn't stand to see Dad get hurt on account of me. The door rattled open. Dad's favorite cologne, Old Spice, filled the bus. Dad's arms closed around me. I don't know whose crying was the loudest.

When I opened my eyes again, at least ten men, some in uniform, poured into the area from the east. Critter led them.

CHAPTER TWENTY-SIX

Dad might have bounded aboard the bus first, but Uncle Ezra came in a close second. Dad swooped me up and hugged me so tight I couldn't get my breath. He used his t-shirt to wipe the wet off my face. Max stuck close, whining a soft whimper of gratitude and licking Dad's hands.

"Momma was here," I told Dad. "Momma took care of me." I couldn't keep the quiver out of my voice. I'd tried to keep bad thoughts out of my head, but when I believed I might lose Dad for that one quick second, I wanted to die too. I wondered if it was wrong to think that way, but your heart scribbles its own words.

Uncle Ezra had Harlan over in the corner of the bus shielding him from everybody's view. I suspected that Harlan finally broke down and cried. He'd been so brave.

The waterworks poured full on from my eyes. I'm not sure anybody had dry eyes right about then. Good gravy, we had been scared to death, stuck in this oven surrounded by robbers!

Max nearly licked Dad to death with more gratitude while we gathered our calm before facing reality. Dad often pushed that face-licking stuff away but tolerated it today.

Surrounding us outside, men in uniform rushed around, looking like they were searching for something. I didn't really care. It was time for me to give up playing detective. Time to leave that up to the people who knew what they were doing. People like Critter.

"Let's get you out of here, Scooter," Dad said.

"What happened? How did you know? Did you catch the robber?" I couldn't stop the questions or the adrenaline.

"Later, Scooter. Let's get you out, get you guys cooled down."

"That's the problem, Dad. I'm stuck. The lift broke." If I hadn't just been saved from possible death, he might've reacted differently, but today, like the face-licking, he tolerated my stupidity really well.

Dad and Uncle Ezra made quick work of getting me off the bus. They got some help and got Zoomster off, too. Someone had rushed water out from an ambulance and paramedics checked all of us, even Max.

Just about that time I saw a sight I never thought I'd see. Gran came scrambling through the woods, her hair flying every which way, and screaming my name at the top of her lungs. If I hadn't still been crying, I'd have laughed my head off.

Gran threw her arms around me like Dad had, as if to have squeezed the life out of me. "You scared us to death. Don't you ever do that again." Her hugs were very welcome today. Tomorrow I'd probably be back to not loving hugs so much, but today they warmed my chill, since I was full-on shivering in the bright sunshine.

An ambulance pulled off the field, and I was thankful none of us were being carried away in it. I didn't know what happened to the three men in the woods, and right now I didn't care.

We all drifted our way back up to the house and left the lawmen to do what they needed to do to clean up the mess I'd made—actually the robber made it, but I might've handled today a little different if I'd had sense enough to predict how it could end.

As we were leaving, Critter told Dad, "Be up to talk to those kids later. Gotta take care of some business first."

I'd never heard his voice so serious. Guess we were in deep trouble. At least I reckon our camera got a picture if anybody tried to dig up the money.

CHAPTER TWENTY-SEVEN

On the way back to the house a butterfly fluttered along in front of us, as if leading the way. When I was little, Momma had always given me butterfly kisses, and told me every single night at bedtime: *No matter how far away from you I am, a butterfly should always remind you that I am with you and love you so much.* And then we'd tickle each other's cheeks with more kisses and giggle our last good nights.

The memory warmed me this time, instead of slicing like a knife. Maybe I could finally let other good memories in—the ones I'd kept locked up tight to avoid the feeling that washed over me like I was being pulled underwater and drowning fast. I hadn't seen Momma's spirit the way I expected. But, on the bus, I'd felt her in the way I'd prayed for. It was like she'd used a key and opened the vault of all my happy memories of her—the ones I'd been afraid to think about, that hurt too much. I'd thought the sorrow was in permanent ink on my soul, but maybe it would get lighter or written over by memories of the happy times.

Sunlight glittered on something on the side of the path. The same path I'd searched that day I was caught outside in the storm. My heart skipped a beat. Harlan saw it at the same time I did.

"A sign," Harlan said. He bent over and picked up my butterfly necklace—the one I thought I'd never see again. He put it around my neck.

"A sign." I patted his hand on my shoulder at the same time I touched my necklace, back in the right place at last. That sign was for Harlan— she'd already shown herself to me.

The rest of the journey home was silent.

I left Harlan with the family for a few minutes while I went to my room with Max.

I needed a chance to remember the warmth of having Momma with me, that total safety I'd been wrapped in on the bus. Even surrounded by the chaos of the banging on the bus, I had wanted that feeling to go on forever. Momma was always in my heart, just like she promised she'd always be. I might not be able to see her, but I felt her as much as I felt Dad's strong hugs with him still here on Earth. And she'd sent us a physical sign, too. Even Harlan, because she let him find it, and put it back in place on my neck.

I took a few more minutes to write some notes in my spirit journal: *When a spirit who's been close to you in life visits, you'll know it. You'll feel like a warmed blanket is covering you, but without touching you. Your heart will settle into a steady rhythm of comfort, like when you used to snuggle your Momma when you were three years old and your biggest worry was whether it would be* Goodnight Moon *or a* Pete the Cat *adventure at bedtime. You'll know, and no one can ever take that away from you. Just like a butterfly kiss, a spirit is barely there, but it's real.*

Momma, this is for you. I understand you told me goodbye today. It's time for your spirit to go to your new home now. We'll be okay. I promise. Butterfly kisses forever!

I knew it was selfish to stay here, but I needed to hang on to this feeling as long as I could. I was afraid that it might be like the mists over the mountains and fade away with light.

Finally, I closed the journal and joined the family in the kitchen. Harlan chomped on some of Gran's cookies as if it were any normal day. Dad and Uncle Ezra might've both wrestled a bear from the looks of them. Gran scurried around the kitchen in her getting-ready-for-dinner-so-don't-bother-me best apron. Her hair rested once again in its normal curls, and her bright lipstick had been recently refreshed. If I didn't know what had just happened in the fields, the kitchen would have felt about right for a Sunday dinner. Normally Dad and Uncle Ezra wouldn't bring that bear-wrestled look to Gran's Sunday dinner table. Today, other than her own immaculate appearance, she seemed to be doing her kitchen thing in a trance, oblivious to the looks of her boys. I suspected that her insides still quivered like Jell-O.

When all eyes turned toward me as I rolled into the kitchen, I wanted to escape to my room again. Time to face the music though. Reckon I'd made a few mistakes along the way and might need to 'fess up. I'd learned a big lesson about making assumptions, and leaving grown-up things to grown-ups, and a big lesson about how brave my best friend was. Most important of all though, I'd felt Momma with me, and recovered my necklace.

"Do you know how close we came to losing one or both of you today? Heat like that can kill someone trapped in a vehicle before they know what hits," Dad finally asked. For once in his life, he kept a huge grin off his face and glared at me and then Harlan. "If Gran hadn't been so worried about you being home alone and sick. If we hadn't come home early . . ."

I worried that the waterworks would start again if I answered. I took a deep breath. I'd never considered that he worried about losing me as much as I worried about losing him.

"I'm sorry. I don't know what else to say. I was trying to make the robber show his face."

"What made you think a robber would show up there?"

"It's a long story." I looked down, hoping I'd get a chance to think about it all before I tried to explain. No such luck. The look Dad drilled me with had me explaining the spirit camera and wanting to catch Momma on film, the loot burial we caught on film instead, and my note to try to catch the robber.

"What I can't understand is *why*. *Why* would you think it was up to you to solve the robberies? *Why* would you put yourself in so much danger?"

"I was mad about Gran getting robbed and hurt. I accidentally caught the robber on the ghost camera. Then when Gran got arrested—"

Gran swung around from the stove, hands on hips, and chimed in, "Good golly molly! I knew I wasn't a robber. That arrest is a story in itself." She actually chuckled.

"At first, Gran, I thought it might be you. You know, all that money." I didn't want to be too specific about that in front of everybody.

"Young lady, he questioned me because he hoped I'd seen the robber when I was with the quilting group, not because he thought I *was* the robber. I got arrested because that robber's money ended up in my till, and all that had to be sorted out. All that money you saw was from my ginseng business—I was trying to get enough together to get you to a special place in Baltimore for therapy. If I weren't so relieved you were safe, why, I'd . . . I'd . . ." Gran turned back to her stove with a final humph and continued to mumble and shake her head for quite a while. She clanged a few pots and pans for extra emphasis. I *knew* she'd be upset to be considered a thief of any kind—at least I was right about that part of it. But, ginseng, when did she start scouring the woods and digging for ginseng again?

I needed a positive change of direction for this conversation. "Did Harlan tell you he wouldn't leave me alone on the bus? He stayed with me when he could've left me behind." I'd never loved Harlan more than when he did that. I still couldn't get over how brave he was—he stayed even though he clearly was terrified.

"Is that right, Harlan?" Dad asked, with such pride in his voice that Harlan beamed.

"She'd have done the same for me." Harlan glanced my way and smiled. "One for all, and all for one."

I hoped I would've, but when you're surrounded by robbers and pouring sweat, mostly you wanted to run. I couldn't run, and I'm not sure what I'd have done if I could have. I hoped I'd be as brave as Harlan had been.

Critter came through the back door. Big

relief. Critter, Dad's friend, not Deputy-on-duty. He walked straight to me and hugged me tight. Then he walked to Harlan and hugged him. Soon enough he had a plate of cookies in front of him with a glass of milk, not seeming at all worried about ruining the dinner we smelled cooking, knowing full well he'd be enjoying some of that too. He and Gran had clearly settled any differences her arrest might've caused.

"Walter confessed everything," Critter said. "We weren't even off your property when he unloaded all his guilty feelings."

"Walter was the robber?" Harlan's eyes widened like saucers. I expected mine might have looked that way too. Our Walter, a robber? "But he's always been so nice!"

"No, no. Walter buried the money for the robber though. The robber, Nick—think you guys call him Panda, had some kind of control over him. Walter owed him a *lot* of money on a gambling debt. Bad thing, that."

"Panda!" At Dad's surprised look I said, "We called Nick Panda because he reminded us of a big old panda bear."

"Critter, can you get to the point? Who was the robber? Only Nick, or Panda, as Scooter calls him? What was Pete doing out there?"

Dad fidgeted and glared at his friend, who was happily stuffing his face with cookies.

"Pete was out there looking after the young ones here. He'd overheard those two, Walter and Nick, hatching up their plan to dig up the cemetery. He put two and two together and trailed them. He knew something was up from Scooter's sign."

"Scooter's sign?" Uncle Ezra stared at me now, all humor gone from his face. Dead-dog serious for once.

"You know. About the cemetery excavation you all are getting ready to do," Critter said.

Dad and Uncle Ezra glanced at each other, then both drilled me with matching blue eyes. Even though I'd mentioned it in my confession, they only now seemed to be processing that I'd set all that up.

I gulped, but nothing helped my suddenly dry-as-a-desert-bone throat. "We . . . I . . . thought we could catch the robbers digging up their loot if we tricked them into thinking there was going to be an excavation of the cemetery."

"And?"

"And we put up a sign at the equipment window. A sign that the cemetery was going to be excavated."

"Okay, back to my story," Critter said, loving his chance to have an audience. "Pete was worried about the young ones here, so he hid in the woods in camouflage and waited. He wasn't going to let anybody hurt those kids of yours. Said he's very fond of Scooter and Harlan, and something about it all worried him, although he didn't have all the pieces to the puzzle." That surprised me, but Harlan just nodded. "Pete had no idea how ugly all of this could get. He didn't know they were stuck on that bus either, at first."

"That's why we saw *three* men in camouflage," I said. "Walter, Nick, and Cr—, uh, Pete. We were so confused."

"Guess we were wrong about him, huh?" Harlan had always hated that nickname, and the minute I found out that Creepy Pete had been the one loaded into the ambulance after getting clobbered trying to protect us, I'd sworn to call him Mr. Pete from now on.

"So, Pete was the one who got hurt, and got carried off in the ambulance. What happened to him?" Dad wanted more answers than he was getting from Critter, who wanted to savor the spin of the tale, like any mountain man. This might be the most excitement he'd ever see as a lawman around here.

"Not sure we have all that sorted out exactly right just yet. Seems like Pete saw Nick notice the kids on the bus and drew the attention to himself. Brave thing to do. Nick clobbered him hard enough to dislocate his shoulder. He's fine though."

"But, why bang all around the bus? With the kids on it?" Dad asked.

"Walter said Nick went wild when he thought he heard someone tracking them in the woods. Then Nick saw some movement on the bus, thought their stalker had hidden there, so tried to scare someone away. Guess when you're up to no good on someone else's property, you don't think too straight."

"So, Nick did all the robberies?" Uncle Ezra asked. He loved a good story almost as much as Critter did. And good for my curiosity he wanted all the details even more than Dad did, so I didn't have to ask.

Uncle Ezra kept glancing at Gran, hoping to get to don his apron, which had never happened when she took over the kitchen for a meal. Or maybe he was worried that the Jell-O in her legs would win and she'd fall over after all.

"We can't prove it just yet, but I expect that's the truth of it. He's not been in the mood to confess, but we have some evidence that might help convince him."

My mouth watered. The smell of fried chicken filled the kitchen. Gran's chicken could win over her worst enemy—if she had any, which I suspected she didn't. No one had eaten any lunch in all the excitement of the day. The feast couldn't come to the table fast enough for me because I hadn't eaten breakfast either in my sick role that morning, and my appetite arrived with the force of a tsunami now that I'd confessed.

Uncle Ezra grabbed a stack of plates and set the table. He set a plate for Critter without asking since Critter had never turned down a meal with us. It meant a lot to me that Uncle Ezra took over my job for this meal because my hands still shook and sweated, and I sure didn't want to make anybody madder by dropping the Sunday china.

Soon enough we had the perfectly set table, the perfectly fried chicken, and my perfectly perfect family and friends around the table.

Gran opened with, "Heavenly Father," and I sighed, expecting it might be one of her long,

long prayers. Instead, Gran said, "Thank you for Pete and his wisdom about the messier-than-a-cow-patty dangers children can get themselves into. Amen." Fastest prayer in the history of Gran.

"Amen," we all said equally as quick, and dug in.

Dad and Uncle Ezra raised milk glasses and gave a cheers-to-Pete salute.

Not much talk took place at that meal. Everyone appreciated the chicken and all the fixings more than they cared about details of the robberies or much small talk while they filled empty bellies. Conversation was more about *pass that please*, or *Gran, you outdid yourself*. The dinner was crowned with Gran's specialty, lemon meringue pie, started at six this morning, before the chaos had erupted. Thankfully, she'd made two! Not even a sliver remained in the dishes when everybody set down their napkins.

"Dad," I said as we put our napkins by our empty plates, "I'm so sorry."

Dad smiled. "Hope you learned a lesson."

I had learned more than one.

"Wait! Maybe we should check the film in the

camera," Harlan said. "We might have caught something on film today."

We went out to the bus. Harlan retrieved the camera and showed Critter what was on it.

Once Critter saw the film, he immediately confiscated my new camera, convinced it had captured enough to force a full confession from Nick, especially after I told him how the figure on Harlan's images matched up to the Dairy Queen robbery films.

"I always had a bad feeling about that man." Critter pointed to the image of Nick. "Once Gran recalled the detail she'd been trying to remember. Nick's voice, arguing with Walter, had sounded familiar to her."

So, Nick had always occupied the #1 spot on the short list of Critter's suspects. But Critter needed actual proof to arrest him, and now he had plenty.

"How'd you kids manage to do all this camera stuff? We can't afford surveillance like this." Critter turned the camera over and examined all the settings.

Dad's face once again had turned grim when he looked at me. All I saw was his disappointment.

CHAPTER TWENTY-EIGHT

Finally, I was in my own room, exhausted. For a while I had wondered if I'd even live through this morning. I wasn't sure why God crammed so much learning into one day. Seems like that was my way of going through life. Plod, plod, WHAM!

I had a few hours to myself before sleep, so I settled in with *The Girl's Ghost Hunting Guide* and read a little, then outlined a new idea for a YouTube episode. It might be fun to hear from viewers about things that connected them to their deceased ancestors, like old pictures, or brushes, or special dishes, or even songs. What it felt like when those things made memories fresh.

When I booted up the computer to start a recording, my video of Zeb appeared, frozen on his tombstone. That still wasn't my screensaver, but it was the same frozen screen I'd seen on the electric night that now seemed like years ago but was only weeks. Over my right shoulder a warmth hovered just behind me. Max, who'd curled around the foot of my wheelchair, glanced up, not at me but higher, over my shoulder, and gave the tiniest yip, like a little hound hello. The now-familiar screen had been speaking to me all along. In the background, behind the headstone, a butterfly hovered. How had I missed that before? Or had I? I touched my necklace, in place again. That same warmth I'd felt on the bus washed over me. Somehow, Momma had broken through for me. It hadn't been her not talking to me all along, but me not knowing how to listen.

I smiled, and sensed I might never see Zeb again, and this was his goodbye. I reckoned his anger was over now—he knew we'd make things right in the cemetery and put his spirit back to rest.

I would film a spirit someday, I would. I'd confirmed their existence enough to make me happy—my heart fairly burst with memories of butterfly kisses and warm spirit hugs.

I got myself ready for bed. I did my standing exercises even though I didn't want to. Stand, count, sit. Stand, count, sit. Maybe soon I'd be able to move my legs forward in a step. I climbed in bed and pulled my covers up.

When Dad came at his usual time to settle me in bed, I smiled from the bed. He stood in the doorway, shook his head. He walked around the room turning off everything as usual.

"Guess you've grown up now, huh?" He sat on the side of my bed. "I'll miss our routine, but I get it."

"I'm going to be okay, Dad. No matter what. I'll be okay."

"I know. Love you, Scooter Marie."

"Love you, too." I squeezed his neck, holding on a long time.

CHAPtER tWENtY-NINE

We started out early on Saturday, all of us, including Gran. We'd prepared a few tokens of appreciation for Zebediah in a time capsule, each of us contributing one thing we treasured to bury in place of the loot, now dug up and mostly returned. Dad had given his favorite blue shirt, Uncle Ezra his best recipe book, I knew the tiny Yoda I'd left Momma a long time ago would enjoy keeping company with another old soul, and Harlan offered some of his best pictures. Gran had written him a letter that she said was too personal to read, but that she felt sure he'd appreciate.

Uncle Ezra, serious for this occasion, said a few words. "Zebediah, we owe you a debt for watching over us, for giving us our home. Thank you for being the man you were who started this little world of ours. Thank you for being sure we got back the money that lets us keep our home, your home."

I knew none of my family had the same feelings I did that spirits were able to hear us, so I appreciated that they did this and believed in me and Zeb. We buried our tokens like the kind of homage ancient Egyptians left for pharaohs. It was the right thing to do to make up for the disrespect he'd suffered.

Then Gran headed out for her quilting, and we headed to work.

Paintball opened on schedule. By the time we arrived at the office, a path of camouflage-covered people swarmed around the doors, waiting for us. Never in the history of my life had people been there before us. The noisy crowd parted to let us through. We'd become famous, and the volume of chatter that surrounded us meant we might make up for some of that money that had been stolen, although Dad got most of it back.

Once we got inside everything looked the same, but somehow it wasn't. It had always felt warm and safe, and now we'd been invaded by something bad. I wanted to do something to bring our good energy back to this place. I pictured Walter, and how much we'd trusted him, had considered him a harmless, friendly guy who tipped big.

Then, something special happened to make it feel good again in there.

Uncle Ezra said, "Look who I found hanging around out there."

Mr. Pete, who'd never again be Creepy Pete, came in and accepted hugs from all of us. Except for Harlan, who shook his hand. Even Max got a little petting.

"I'm sorry, Mr. Pete, that I got you hurt." I didn't think I could ever make it up to him. His shoulder area looked lumpy, like he had bandages under his clothes. His plain old t-shirt showed he wasn't up to paintball yet, or he'd have been wearing his camo.

Harlan added his apologies.

"I couldn't stand knowing those men might be up to no good. And I thought you might be too young to understand how bad they were," Pete said. "I'd have gotten the law if I'd realized how bad they really were. I never expected you kids to be stuck on that bus."

That was the most words he'd ever spoken, all at one time.

Dad pumped his hand again, "You did right, Pete. You're VIP around here from now on. Never allowed to pay again."

Uncle Ezra pumped Pete's hand like an old-fashioned well pump. He might be getting tired of all those hands pumping, even if it was his good arm. "We put together a little something for you." He handed Pete a bundle of the best of everything we carried at the store.

A silence hung in the air, but it wasn't awkward, just thoughtful, like we all wanted to remember a special moment.

Pete's eyes got a little leaky looking and he bowed his head for a minute. "I thank you." And then he disappeared out the door as quickly as we were used to seeing him come and go.

We followed after him. Dad wasn't much for speechifying, but he signaled for attention to say a few words to the waiting crowd.

"Thanks for coming out today to show your support. This is the kind of support that makes us proud to be hill people. We appreciate it. This is a bigger crowd than usual, so we hope you'll be patient while we get you set up. Everyone here today will get a bonus bag of paintballs, and we'll extend playing hours until dusk so you can get your money's worth. Have fun!"

As soon as they all left for the fields, I showed Harlan the video I'd just seen about an awesome haunted cemetery in St. Louis. Maybe we could talk Uncle Ezra into a road trip.